GARBAGE GAMES
LANGUAGE & MATH GAMES
USING RECYCLED CONTAINERS

WRITTEN BY BETTY ISAAK
ILLUSTRATED BY BEV ARMSTRONG

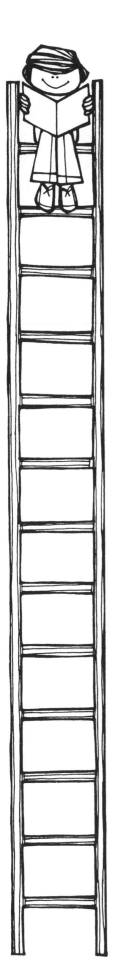

The Learning Works

The purchase of this book entitles the individual teacher to reproduce copies for use in the classroom.

The reproduction of any part for an entire school or school system or for commercial use is strictly prohibited.

No form of this work may be reproduced or transmitted or recorded without written permission from the publisher.

Contents

Skill	**Game**

Phonics

Grammar

Contents
(continued)

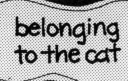 

belonging to the cat   Monday   Mon.

Contents (continued)

Math

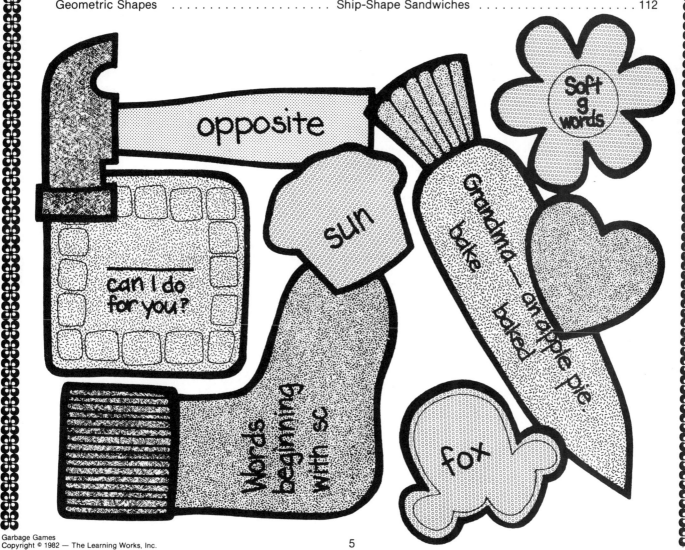

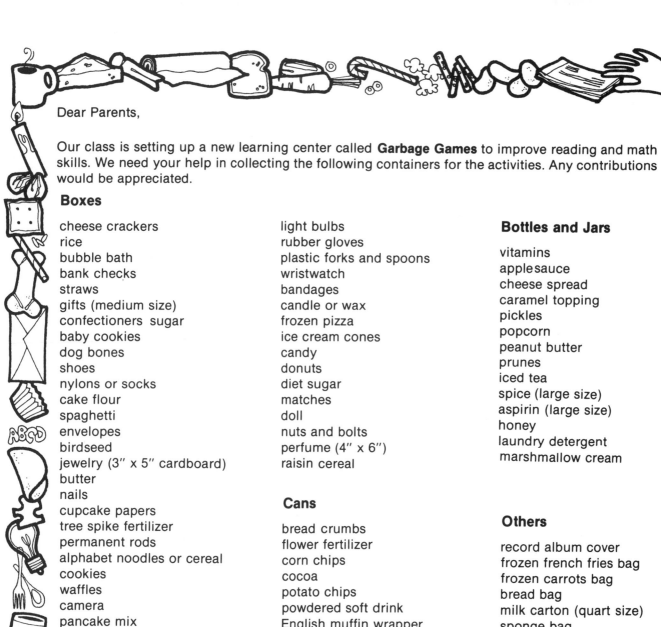

Dear Parents,

Our class is setting up a new learning center called **Garbage Games** to improve reading and math skills. We need your help in collecting the following containers for the activities. Any contributions would be appreciated.

Boxes

cheese crackers
rice
bubble bath
bank checks
straws
gifts (medium size)
confectioners sugar
baby cookies
dog bones
shoes
nylons or socks
cake flour
spaghetti
envelopes
birdseed
jewelry (3" x 5" cardboard)
butter
nails
cupcake papers
tree spike fertilizer
permanent rods
alphabet noodles or cereal
cookies
waffles
camera
pancake mix
stationery
painting kit
quick-cooking oatmeal
shoe polish
snack food
frozen fish
wax paper
aluminum foil
crayons
taco shells
graham crackers
ice cream (half-gallon size)
frozen dinners
fruit cereal
puzzles
french toast
paper cups

light bulbs
rubber gloves
plastic forks and spoons
wristwatch
bandages
candle or wax
frozen pizza
ice cream cones
candy
donuts
diet sugar
matches
doll
nuts and bolts
perfume (4" x 6")
raisin cereal

Cans

bread crumbs
flower fertilizer
corn chips
cocoa
potato chips
powdered soft drink
English muffin wrapper
salad croutons
coffee
clay
lemonade
bouillon
pretzels

Plastic Containers

cottage cheese
yogurt
margarine
whipped topping
ketchup
syrup
coleslaw
sour cream

Bottles and Jars

vitamins
applesauce
cheese spread
caramel topping
pickles
popcorn
peanut butter
prunes
iced tea
spice (large size)
aspirin (large size)
honey
laundry detergent
marshmallow cream

Others

record album cover
frozen french fries bag
frozen carrots bag
bread bag
milk carton (quart size)
sponge bag
child's pencil bag
cosmetic bag
egg carton
clothespin bag
child's lunch box
plastic bag (zip-lock top)
salt carton

Sincerely,

_____

GARBAGE GAME WHIZ KID AWARD

PRESENTED TO

_____

WHO HAS SUCCESSFULLY PLAYED

_____

GARBAGE GAMES

_____
GARBAGE GAME COACH
_____
DATE

Vitamin Vowels

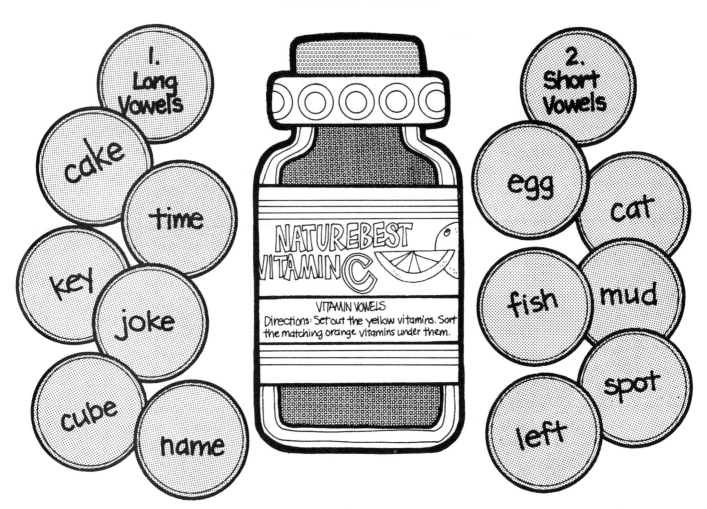

Container: vitamin bottle

Materials: yellow and orange paper

Preparation:
1. Cut out two yellow and twenty orange circles one and one-half inches in diameter.
2. On one yellow circle write **Long Vowels**, and on the other write **Short Vowels**. Number these **1** and **2**.
3. On the orange circles write words containing long or short vowels.

    Suggested word list:

cake	*time*	*cat*	*sit*
name	*joke*	*hand*	*lost*
be	*rope*	*egg*	*spot*
key	*cube*	*left*	*but*
ice	*mule*	*fish*	*mud*

4. For self-checking, number the backs of the orange circles to match the yellow ones.

Directions: Set out the yellow vitamins. Sort the matching orange vitamins under them.

Apple Answers

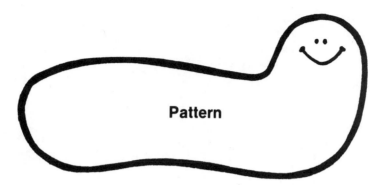

Pattern

Container: applesauce jar

Materials: red, green, and white paper

Preparation:
1. Using the patterns, cut out one red apple and one green worm.
2. Cut eighteen white strips, each measuring one inch by four inches.
3. On the apple write **Sounds like the a in apple**, and on the worm write **Sounds like the a in cake**. Number these **1** and **2**.
4. On the strips write words that contain long and short **a**.

   Suggested word list:

bad	mad	rat	baby	late	say
dad	man	sad	came	made	table
had	mat	wag	flake	paint	whale

5. For self-checking, number the backs of the white strips to match the apple or worm.

Directions: Set out the apple and worm. Sort the matching white word strips under them.

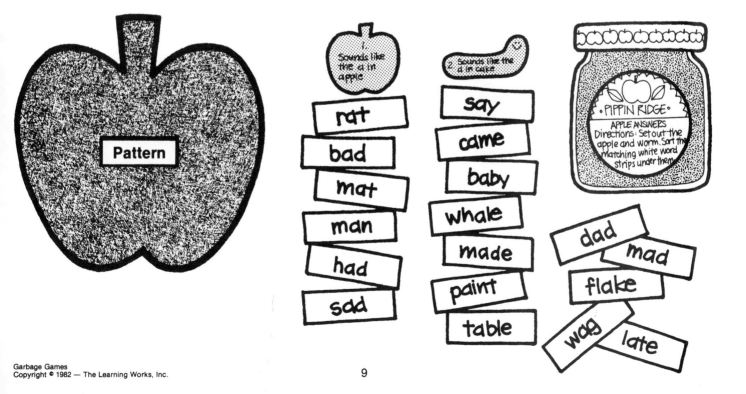

Cheese Please

Container: cheese jar or cheese cracker box

Material: yellow paper

Preparation:
1. Cut out twenty circles two inches in diameter and two two-inch squares.

2. On one square write **Sounds like the e in bed**, and on the other write **Sounds like the e in cheese**. Number these **1** and **2**.

3. On the circles write words containing long and short **e**.

   Suggested word list:

beg	net	bean	mean
bent	pen	beet	meet
fed	send	feel	peas
jet	set	green	please
met	tell	leaf	seat

4. For self-checking, number the backs of the cheese circles to match the cheese squares.

Directions: Set out the cheese squares. Sort the matching round cheeses under them.

Twice as Rice

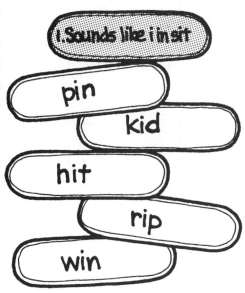

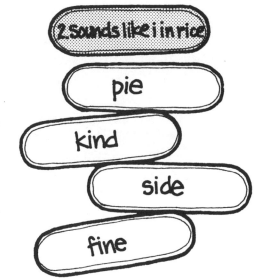

Container: rice box

Materials: white and brown paper

Preparation:
1. Using the pattern, cut out two brown and twenty white grains of rice.
2. On one brown grain write **Sounds like the i in sit** and on the other write **Sounds like the i in rice**. Number these **1** and **2**.
3. On the white grains write words containing long and short i.

   Suggested word list:

bit	kid	rip	kind	side
dig	lip	win	line	sign
fin	mitt	dine	pie	time
hit	pin	fine	ride	vine

4. For self-checking, number the backs of the white grains of rice to match the brown grains of rice.

Directions: Set out the brown grains of rice. Sort the matching white grains of rice under them.

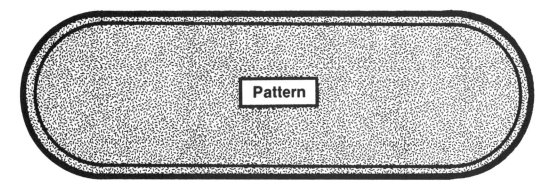

Pattern

Tops in Pops

Container: record album cover

Materials: black and white paper

Preparation:
1. Using the patterns, cut out two black records and two white record labels.
2. Cut twenty strips of white paper, each measuring one inch by three inches.
3. Glue the white labels onto the records.
4. On one label write **Sounds like the o in pop,** and on the other write **Sounds like the o in boat.** Number these **1** and **2**.
5. On the strips write words containing long and short **o**.
   Suggested word list:

clock	not	bowl	home
cot	pond	coal	note
got	rod	coat	road
hot	rot	foam	toe
mom	stop	hole	vote

6. For self-checking, number the backs of the strips to match the records.

Directions: Set out the records. Sort the matching word strips under them.

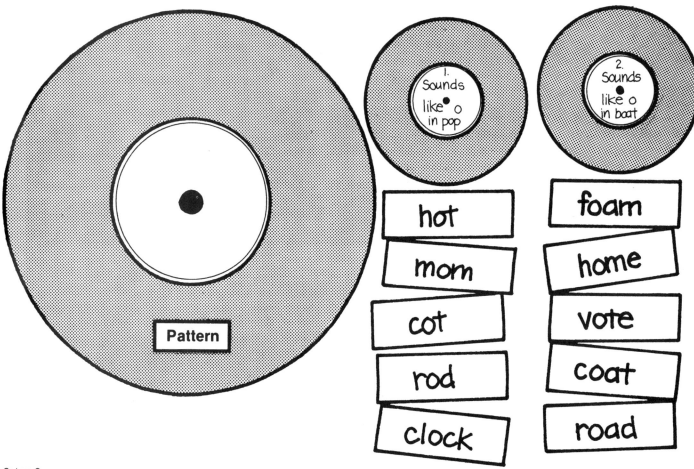

Pattern

1.
Sounds like o in pop

2.
Sounds like o in boat

hot
mom
cot
rod
clock

foam
home
vote
coat
road

Crumble Up

Container: bread crumb can

Materials: blue and white paper

Preparation:
1. Using the patterns, cut out two blue birds and twenty white bread crumbs.
2. On one bird write **Sounds like the u in cup**, and on the other write **Sounds like the u in cube**. Number these **1** and **2**.
3. On the bread crumbs write words containing long and short **u**.

   Suggested word list:

but	gum	such	glue	tube
cub	hut	sun	mule	tune
cuff	number	blue	ruin	use
cut	run	cute	suit	vacuum

4. For self-checking, number the backs of the bread crumbs to match the birds.

Directions: Set out the birds. Sort the matching bread crumbs under them.

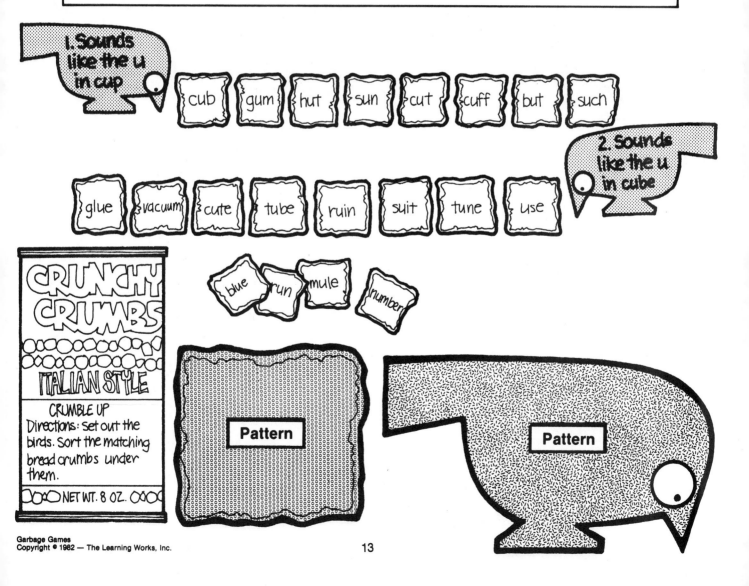

Yummy Yogurt

Container: strawberry yogurt carton

Materials: red and green paper

Preparation:

1. Using the patterns, cut out twenty red strawberries and two green leaves.

2. On one leaf write **y sounds like i**, and on the other write **y sounds like e**. Number these **1** and **2**.

3. On the strawberries write words ending in **y**.

Suggested word list:

buy	fry	spy	candy	honey
by	my	try	family	puppy
cry	shy	baby	funny	sadly
dry	sly	bunny	happy	slowly

4. For self-checking, number the backs of the strawberries to match the leaves.

Directions: Set out the two leaves. Sort the matching strawberries under them.

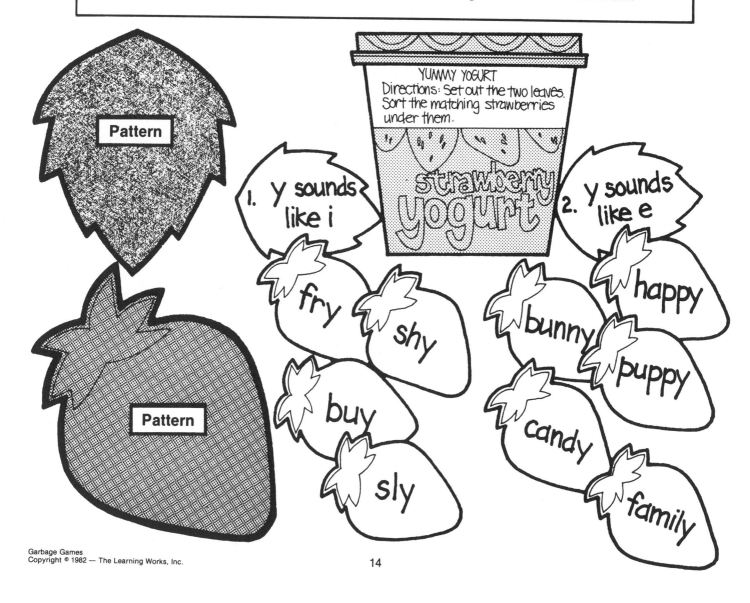

Oodles of Noodles

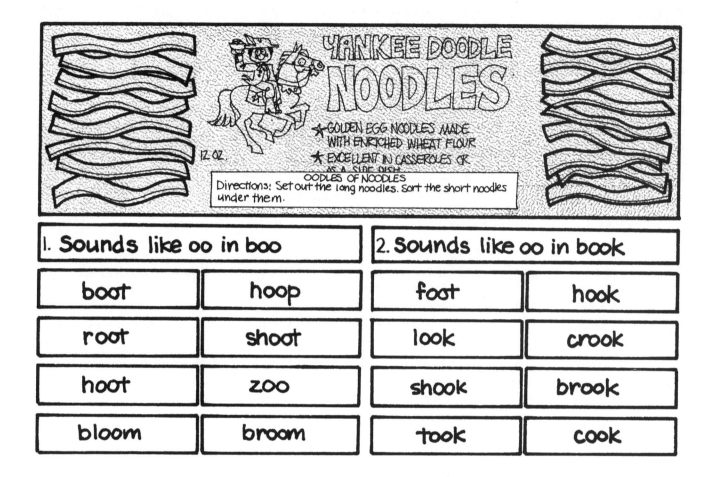

1. Sounds like oo in boo

boot	hoop
root	shoot
hoot	zoo
bloom	broom

2. Sounds like oo in book

foot	hook
look	crook
shook	brook
took	cook

Container: noodle box

Material: white paper

Preparation:

1. From the paper, cut two long noodles, each measuring one inch by eight inches, and twenty short noodles, each measuring one inch by two inches.

2. On one of the long noodles write **Sounds like oo in boo**, and on the other long noodle write **Sounds like oo in book**. Number these **1** and **2**.

3. On each of the short noodles, write a word containing **oo**.

   Suggested word list:

book	foot	shook	boot	room
brook	hook	took	broom	root
cook	look	bloom	hoop	shoot
crook	nook	boo	hoot	zoo

4. For self-checking, number the backs of the short noodles to match the long ones.

Directions: Set out the long noodles. Sort the short noodles under them.

Born from Corn

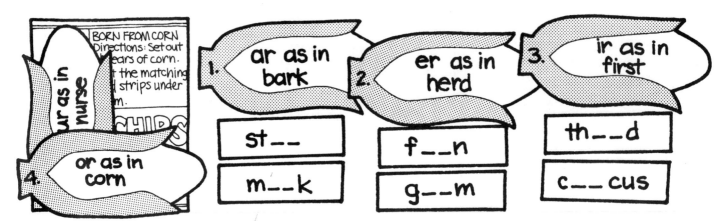

Container: corn chip can

Materials: yellow paper and green crayon or colored pen

Preparation:
1. Using the pattern, cut out five ears of corn. Then, cut out twenty strips of paper, each measuring one inch by three inches.
2. Color the husks on the ears of corn.
3. On each ear of corn write one of the following: **ar as in bark, er as in herd, ir as in first, or as in corn,** or **ur as in nurse.** Number these **1** through **5.**
4. On the strips write words in these categories, omitting these letters in each word.

   Suggested word list:

far	fern	bird	for	burn
mark	germ	circus	more	hurry
part	jerk	fir	store	purse
star	perk	third	tore	turn

5. For self-checking, number the backs of the word strips to match the ears of corn.

Directions: Set out the ears of corn. Sort the matching word strips under them.

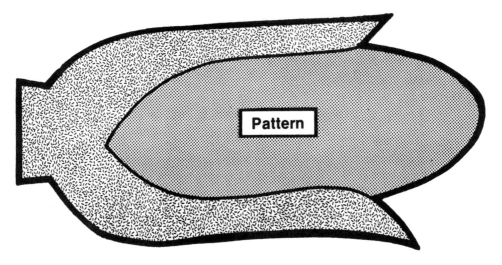

Pattern

Cottage Cheese Consonants

COTTAGE CHEESE CONSONANTS

Directions: Line up the cottage cheese shapes.
Find a correct consonant for each shape.
Some may use more than one consonant.

Container: cottage cheese carton

Material: white paper

Preparation:
1. Using the pattern, cut out twenty cottage cheese shapes. Then, cut twenty one-inch squares.
2. On each cottage cheese shape write a word, but leave off the initial consonant.

   Suggested word list:

boat	game	love	quiet	vowel
cow	house	mouse	race	want
daddy	jet	nail	said	yard
face	kitten	play	take	zoo

3. On the squares write the missing consonant(s).
4. For self-checking, write the consonant(s) on the back of each cottage cheese shape.

Directions: Line up the cottage cheese shapes. Find a correct consonant for each shape. Some may use more than one consonant.

Pattern

PHONICS
CONSONANTS—BLENDS AND DIGRAPHS

Check It Out

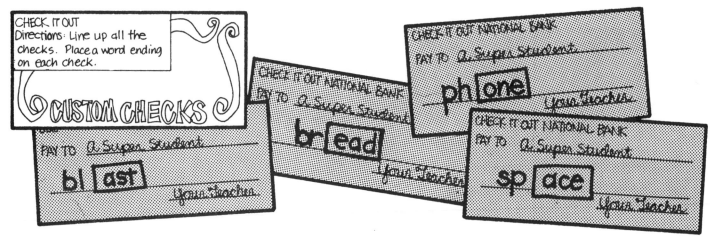

Container: bank check box

Material: yellow paper

Preparation:
1. Using the pattern, cut out and mark twenty-one checks.
2. Cut twenty-one strips of paper, each measuring one inch by three inches.
3. Write a consonant digraph on the money line of each check, allowing room for the remainder of a word.
4. Write word endings on the strips corresponding to the digraphs.

   Suggested word list:

blast	close	flurry	phone	slouch	spooky	tractor
bread	crayon	friend	present	smelly	story	twist
cherry	drape	plaster	shadow	snarl	swish	write

5. For self-checking, write the words on the backs of the word strips.

Directions: Line up all the checks. Place a word ending on each check.

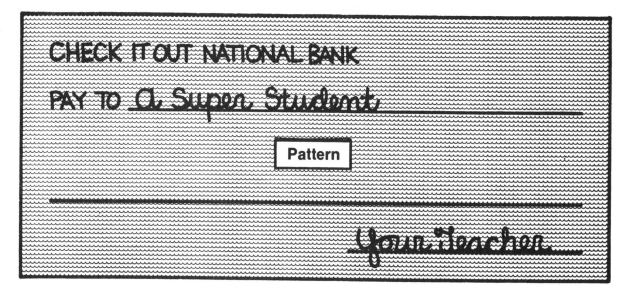

Bright Blue Bubbles

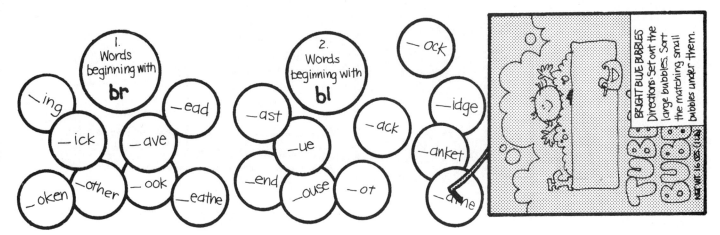

Container:	bubble bath box
Material:	blue paper
Preparation:	1. Using the patterns, cut out two large and twenty small bubbles.

2. On one large bubble write **Words beginning with br**, and on the other write **Words beginning with bl**. Number these **1** and **2**.

3. On the small bubbles write words that begin with **bl** or **br**, omitting these letters.

Suggested word list:

black	blast	blouse	break	brook
blame	blend	blue	brick	brother
blank	block	brave	bright	brown
blanket	blot	bread	broken	brush

4. For self-checking, number the backs of the small bubbles to match the large ones.

Directions: Set out the large bubbles. Sort the matching small bubbles under them.

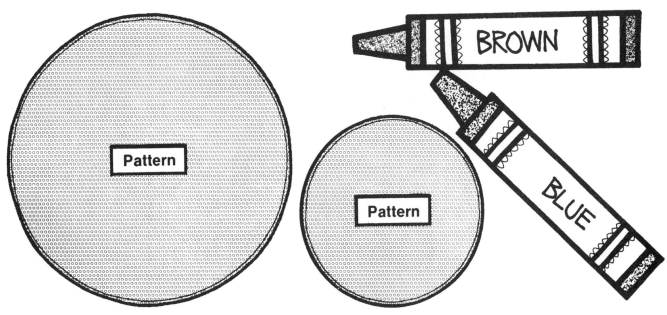

Drink, Drank, Drunk

DRINK, DRANK, DRUNK
Directions: Line up all the straws.
Put a disk on the word that
fits the sentence

SUPER
SIPPER

SODA
STRAWS
WITH A BUILT-IN BEND
100 STRAWS

The flowers began to—. draw droop

Father used his —. drill drape

Don't — the vase. drip drop

There was only one — in the band. drum drag

Mother bought a new —. drop dress

The clothes were almost —. dry drip

Mary's ice cream _____. dripped draw

We had a — of ice water. drink drank

Container: drinking straw box

Materials: yellow paper and clear plastic bingo disks

Preparation:
1. Using the pattern, cut out ten straws.
2. Write a sentence using a word with a **dr** digraph on each straw, omitting that word.
3. Write two word choices at the end of each sentence.

   Suggested sentence list:

   We had a _____ of ice water.   drink drank
   Bill _____ the car very carefully.   driven drove
   Mary's ice cream _____ .   dripped draw
   Father used his _____ .   drill drape
   Mother bought a new _____ .   drop dress
   Don't _____ the new vase.   drop drip
   Mark had a _____ last night.   dream drum
   The clothes were almost _____ .   dry drip
   There was only one _____ in the band.   drum drag
   The flowers began to _____ .   draw droop

4. For self-checking, write the correct word on the back of each straw.

Directions: Line up all the straws. Put a disk on the word that fits the sentence.

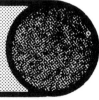

Pattern

Flavorful French Fries

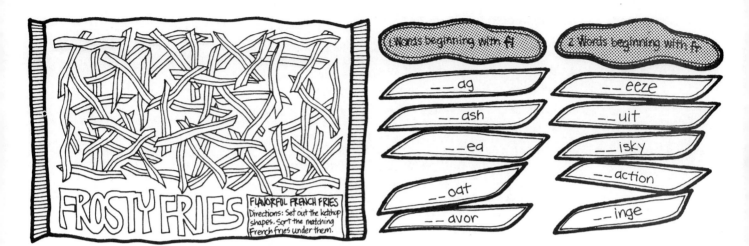

Container: frozen french fries box or bag

Materials: yellow and red paper

Preparation:
1. Using the patterns, cut out two red ketchup shapes and twenty yellow french fries.
2. On one ketchup shape write **Words beginning with fl**, and on the other write **Words beginning with fr**. Number these **1** and **2**.
3. On the french fries write words that begin with the digraphs **fl** or **fr**, omitting these letters.

   Suggested word list:

flag	flip	flower	freeze	from
flash	float	fluffy	friend	frost
flavor	flood	fraction	fringe	frozen
flea	flow	freedom	frisky	fruit

4. For self-checking, number the backs of the french fries to match the ketchup shapes.

Directions: Set out the ketchup shapes. Sort the matching french fries under them.

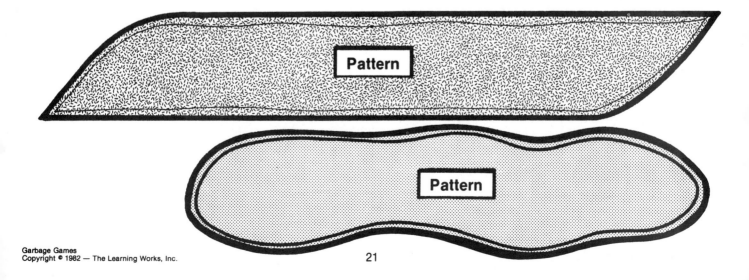

Bony Blends

Container: dog bone box

Materials: white paper and clear plastic bingo disks

Preparation:
1. Using the pattern, cut out twelve bones.
2. On each bone, write a sentence with a word that contains an **L** digraph.
3. Write two word choices at the end of each sentence.

   Suggested sentence list:

   The car was very _____ .   slam slow
   John knew it was time to _____ .   slip sleep
   Put the food on your _____ .   plate plant
   Please keep your _____ in line.   plan place
   I used _____ to hold the paper together.   glue glow
   I'd like a _____ of milk.   globe glass
   We raised the _____ in the morning.   flip flag
   The fire has bright _____ .   flows flames
   He is a boy in our _____ .   class clean
   Please _____ the door all the way.   clap close
   He had a warm _____ on his bed.   blanket bloom
   Last night we felt the icy _____ of the wind.   blasts blisters

4. For self-checking, write the correct word on the back of the bone.

Directions: Line up all the bones. Put a disk on the word that fits the sentence.

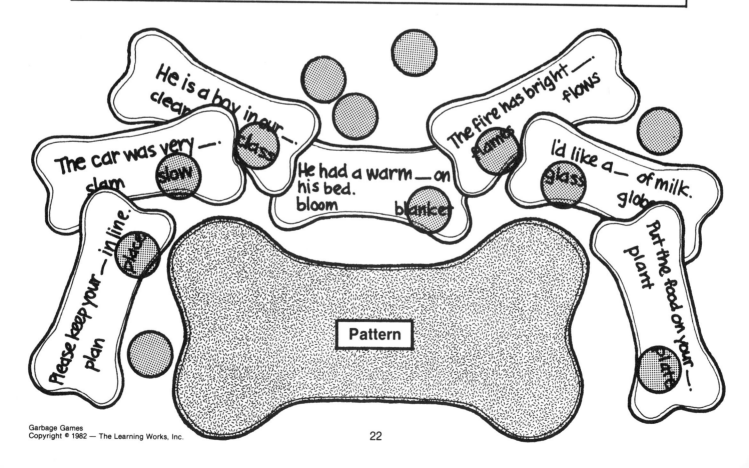

Pleasant Presents

Container: gift box with bow

Materials: paper in assorted colors (including yellow) and crayons or colored pens

Preparation:
1. Using the patterns, cut out three yellow gift boxes and fifteen bows in assorted colors.
2. Color the bows on the gift boxes.
3. On each box write one of the following: **Words beginning with ph**, **Words beginning with pl**, or **Words beginning with pr**. Number these **1**, **2**, and **3**.
4. On the cutout bows write words beginning with **ph**, **pl**, and **pr**, omitting these digraphs in each word.

   Suggested word list:

phonics	physical	plate	promise
phonograph	place	plum	protect
phony	plain	present	prove
photograph	plant	program	prune

5. For self-checking, number the backs of the bows to match the gift boxes.

Directions: Set out the three gift boxes. Sort the matching bows under them.

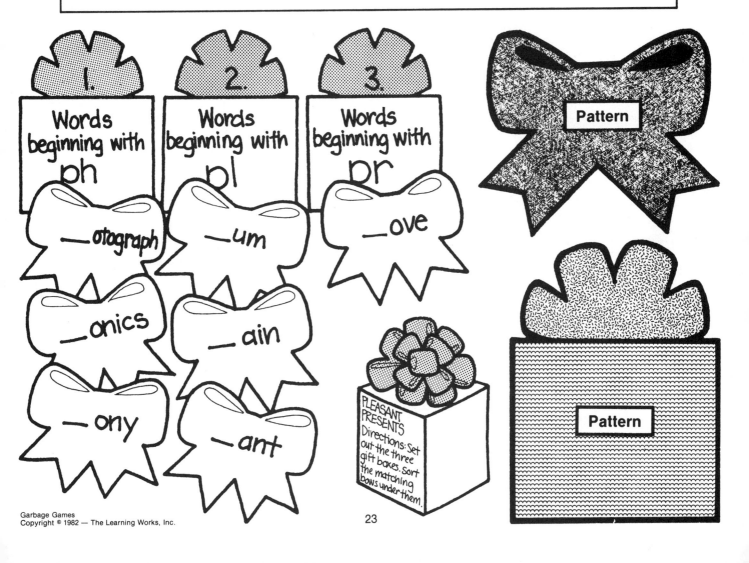

Super Sweets

Container: confectioners sugar box

Materials: pink and white paper

Preparation: 1. Using the pattern, cut out nine pink candy drops and twenty-seven white ones.

2. On each pink candy drop, write one of the following: **Words beginning with sc, Words beginning with sh, Words beginning with sk, Words beginning with sl, Words beginning with sm, Words beginning with sn, Words beginning with sp, Words beginning with st,** or **Words beginning with sw.** Number these **1** through **9.**

3. On the white candy drops, write words that begin with **sc, sh, sk, sl, sm, sn, sp, st,** and **sw,** omitting the opening consonant digraph in each word.

   Suggested word list:

scale	*skillet*	*smooth*	*steal*
scar	*skull*	*snail*	*stood*
scrape	*sliver*	*snarl*	*study*
sharp	*slouch*	*sneeze*	*swallow*
should	*slush*	*space*	*swing*
shrink	*smile*	*special*	*swirl*
ski	*smog*	*splash*	

4. For self-checking, number the white candy drops to match the pink candy drops.

Directions: Set out the pink candy drops. Sort the white candy drops under them.

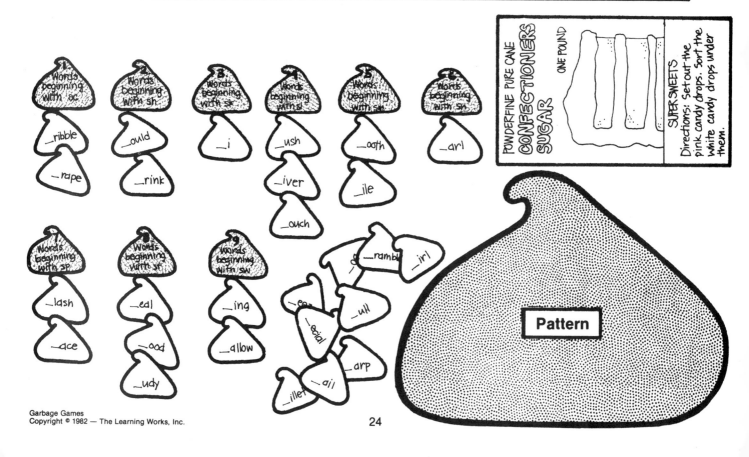

Twins or Triplets

Container: baby cookie box

Materials: pink and blue paper

Preparation:
1. Using the patterns, cut out and mark one pink rattle, one blue rattle, and twenty pink baby faces.
2. On one rattle write **Words beginning with tr**, and on the other write **Words beginning with tw**. Number these **1** and **2**.
3. On the faces write words that begin with **tw** or **tr**, omitting these digraphs in each word.

   Suggested word list:

track	trick	trust	twig
trail	trim	tweet	twin
trap	trip	twelve	twine
treat	trot	twenty	twinkle
tree	truck	twice	twirl

4. For self-checking, number the backs of the faces to match the rattles.

Directions: Set out the rattles. Sort the matching baby faces under them.

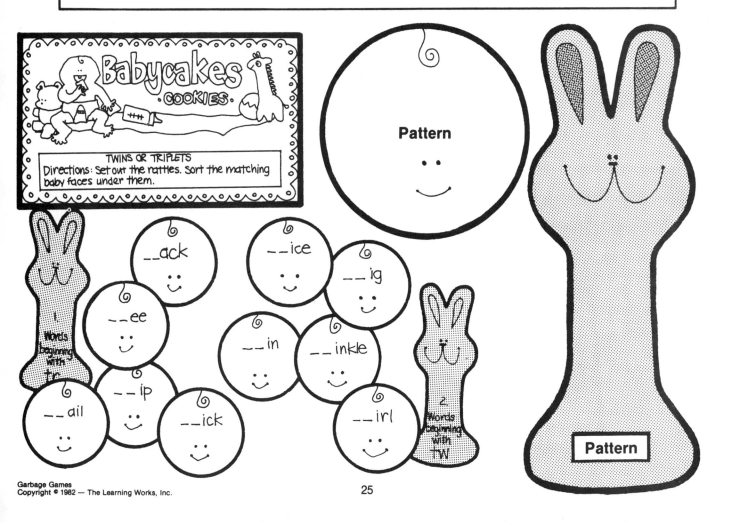

Choose a Shoe

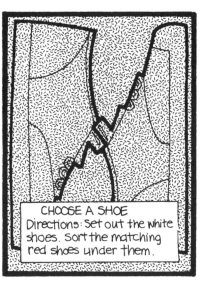

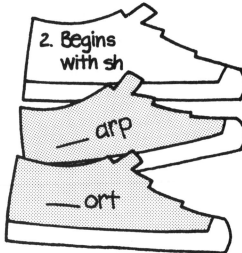

Container: shoe box

Materials: red and white paper

Preparation:
1. Using the pattern, cut out and mark two white and twenty red shoes.
2. On one white shoe write **Begins with ch**, and on the other write **Begins with sh**.
3. On ten red shoes write words that begin with **ch**, and on the other ten write words beginning with **sh**, omitting these letters in each word.

Suggested word list:

chain	cheap	chose	sharp	shoe
chair	cheek	church	sheet	short
chance	child	shadow	shine	shower
chap	chip	shape	shirt	shut

4. For self-checking, number the backs of the red shoes to match the corresponding white shoes.

Directions: Set out the white shoes. Sort the matching red shoes under them.

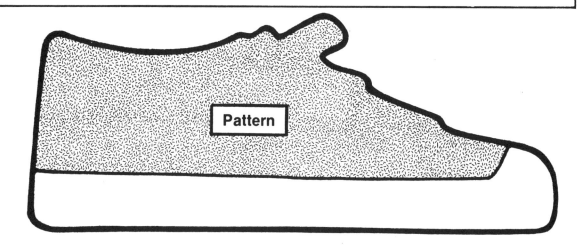

Pattern

Pick a Pickle

Container: pickle jar

Materials: light and dark green paper

Preparation:
1. Using the pattern, cut out two light green and twenty dark green pickles.
2. On one light green pickle write **P sounds like p in pet**, and on the other write **Ph sounds like f in phone**. Number these **1** and **2**.
3. On the dark green pickles, write the words that begin with **p** and **ph**.

Suggested word list:

page	people	pinch	phone	photograph
pan	pet	pond	phonics	phrase
party	pill	phantom	phonograph	physician
past	pillow	pheasant	phony	physical

4. For self-checking, number the backs of the dark pickles to match the light pickles.

Directions: Set out the light green pickles. Sort the matching dark green pickles under them.

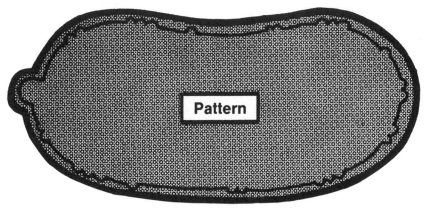

Pattern

Caramel Centers

Container: caramel syrup jar

Materials: white and brown paper, Popsicle sticks, white glue, and crayons or marking pens

Preparation:
1. Using the pattern, cut out two white candy circles.
2. Color them and glue each to a Popsicle stick to make two lollipops.
3. On one lollipop write **Hard c words** and on the other lollipop write **Soft c words**. Number these **1** and **2**.
4. Using the pattern, cut out twenty brown caramel centers.
5. On each caramel center, write a word containing a hard or soft **c**.

   Suggested word list:

cabin	cap	cell	mice
cake	clock	cent	nice
came	coat	face	pencil
camel	cuff	fence	race
candle	cup	lace	rice

6. For self-checking, number the caramel centers to match the lollipops.

Directions: Set out the lollipops. Sort the matching caramel centers under them.

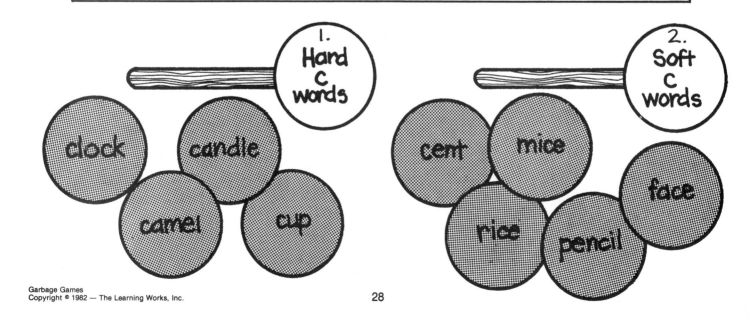

On the Grow

Container: plant fertilizer can

Materials: orange and green paper

Preparation:
1. Using the pattern, cut out two orange flowers. Then, cut out twenty green strips of paper each measuring one inch by three inches.
2. On one flower write **Soft g words**, and on the other write **Hard g words**. Number these **1** and **2**.
3. On the green strips write words containing hard or soft **g**.

   Suggested word list:

age	edge	huge	game	gold
bridge	gem	page	gave	good
budge	giant	dog	goat	gun
cage	gym	egg	goes	rag

4. For self-checking, number the backs of the strips to match the flowers.

Directions: To make the flowers grow, set out the flowers and put the matching stems under them.

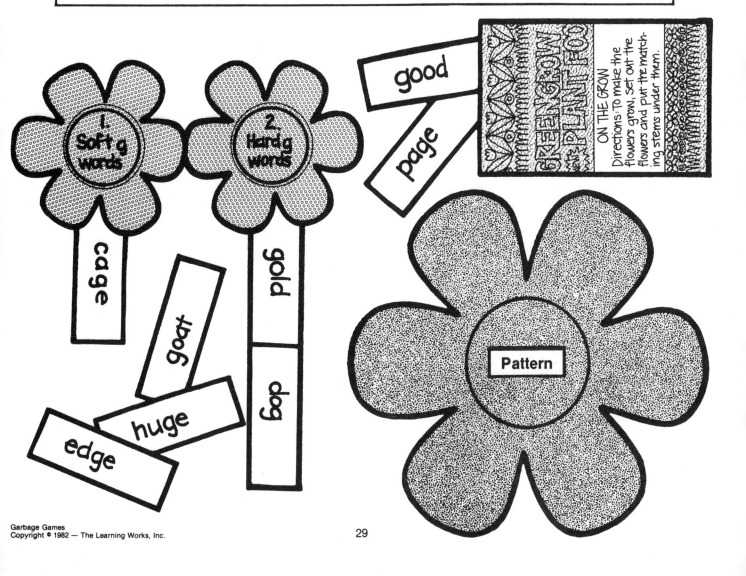

Chocolate Choices

Container:	cocoa can
Materials:	light brown paper and clear plastic bingo disks
Preparation:	1. Cut ten strips of paper, each measuring two inches by four inches.

2. Write a sentence about chocolate on each strip.

   Suggested sentence list:

   Chocolate pudding is really good.
   Chocolate cookies and donuts are both round.
   We ate chocolate brownies.
   Chocolate grasshoppers have a different taste.
   I love chocolate milk.
   Chocolate candy is my favorite.
   Chocolate sodas are made with ice cream.
   Do you like chocolate cake?
   Mother used chocolate frosting.
   Chocolate caramels are chewy.

3. For self-checking, write the noun(s) on the back of each strip.

Directions: Line up the chocolate sentences. Place a disk on every noun.

Vegetable Verbs

Container: frozen carrot bag

Materials: orange paper, clear plastic bingo disks, and green crayon or colored pen

Preparation:
1. Using the pattern, cut out fifteen carrots.
2. Color the carrot tops.
3. On each carrot write a sentence, omitting the verb.

   Suggested sentence list:

   Mark _____ down the street.   ran run
   The teacher _____ her papers.   mark marked
   Jan _____ her cup with milk.   fill filled
   The boat can _____ down the stream.   floated float
   Jill _____ home from school.   came come
   The dog _____ at the cat.   barked barking
   The pig _____ on the farm.   live lived
   Bill _____ the ball very hard.   hitting hit
   We all _____ a mile yesterday.   walked walk
   The cat _____ up the tree.   climb climbed
   The whole class can _____ that song.   sing sang
   All the children were _____ .   play playing
   The red plane _____ very high.   flew fly
   Grandma _____ an apple pie.   bake baked
   The magician _____ a rabbit out of his hat.   took take

4. For self-checking, put a dot on the back of the carrot indicating the position of the correct verb.

Directions: Line up all the carrots. Place a disk on the right verb for each sentence.

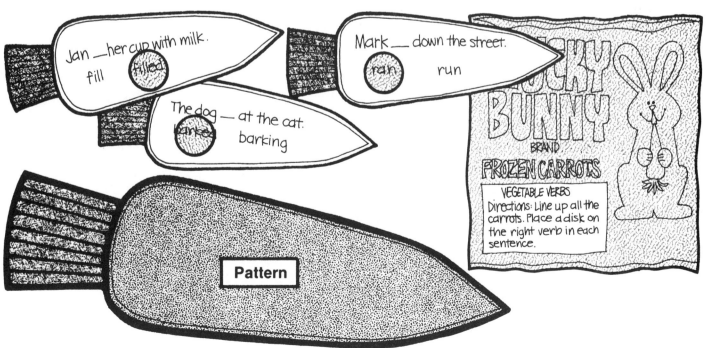

Pattern

Syrupy Sentences

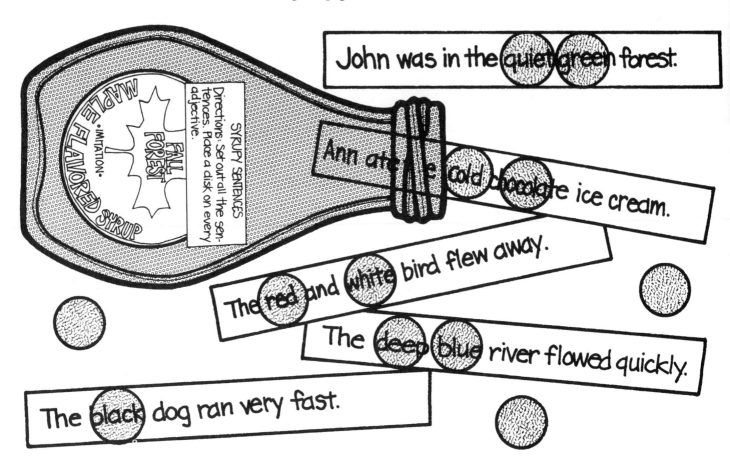

Container: syrup bottle

Materials: white paper and clear plastic bingo disks

Preparation: 1. Cut ten strips of paper, each measuring one-half inch by eight inches.

2. Write a sentence containing at least one adjective on each strip.

   Suggested sentence list:

   The deep blue river flowed quickly.
   The red and white bird flew away.
   The dark brown monkey was jumping.
   The black dog ran very fast.
   Ann ate the cold chocolate ice cream.
   The short fat man smiled.
   John was in the quiet green forest.
   The angry old man yelled at the children.
   The large brown bear ran into the woods.
   Our red, white, and blue flag is beautiful.

3. For self-checking, write the adjective(s) on the back of each strip.

Directions: Set out all the sentences. Place a disk on every adjective.

Ketchup Quickly

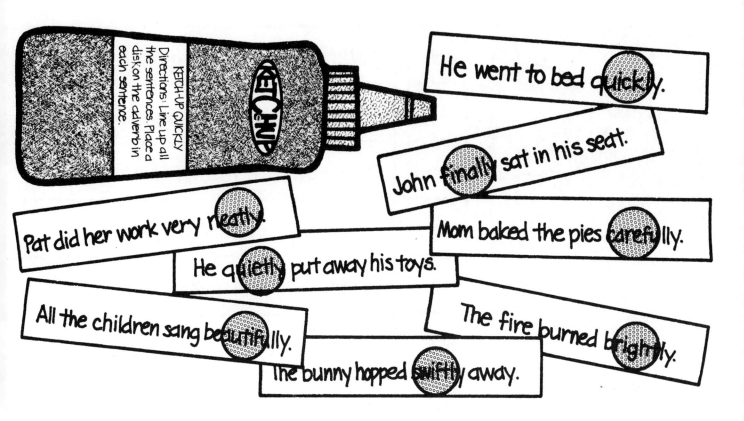

Container: ketchup container

Materials: red paper and clear plastic bingo disks

Preparation: 1. Cut twelve strips of red paper, each measuring one inch by five inches.

2. Write a sentence that contains an adverb on each strip.

Suggested sentence list:

He went to bed quickly.
He quietly put away his toys.
Mom baked the pies carefully.
The turtle crawled slowly on the rock.
All the children sang beautifully.
John walked shyly onto the stage.
The nurse treated me kindly.
Jenny sang sweetly in the play.
The bunny hopped swiftly away.
The fire burned brightly.
John finally sat in his seat.
Pat did her work neatly.

3. For self-checking, write the adverb on the back of each strip.

Directions: Line up all the sentences. Place a disk on the adverb in each sentence.

Potato Chip Pronouns

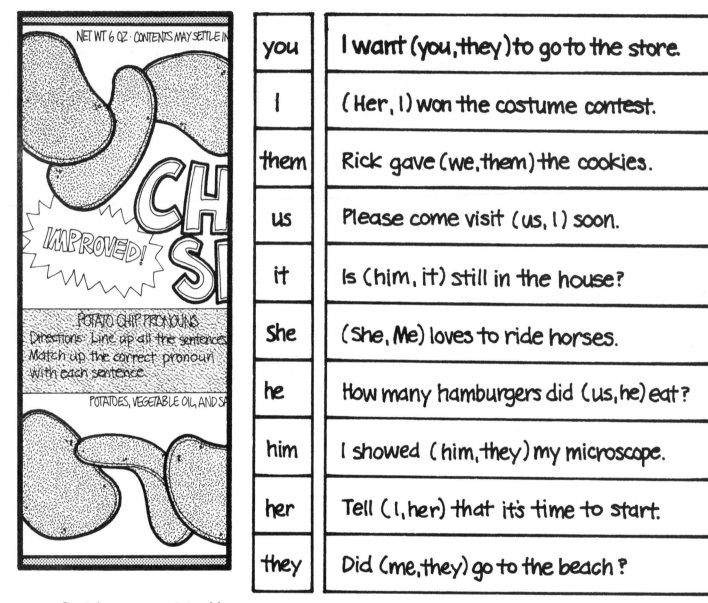

you	I want (you, they) to go to the store.
I	(Her, I) won the costume contest.
them	Rick gave (we, them) the cookies.
us	Please come visit (us, I) soon.
it	Is (him, it) still in the house?
She	(She, Me) loves to ride horses.
he	How many hamburgers did (us, he) eat?
him	I showed (him, they) my microscope.
her	Tell (I, her) that it's time to start.
they	Did (me, they) go to the beach?

Container: potato chip can

Material: yellow paper

Preparation:
1. Cut ten strips of yellow paper, each measuring one inch by eight inches. Then, cut ten rectangles, each measuring one inch by two inches.
2. Write one of the pronouns **he**, **she**, **they**, **it**, **you**, **I**, **them**, **us**, or **her** on each rectangle.
3. Write a sentence containing a pronoun on each strip.
4. For self-checking, number the backs of matching strips and rectangles.

Directions: Line up all the sentences. Match up the correct pronoun with each sentence.

And But-ter

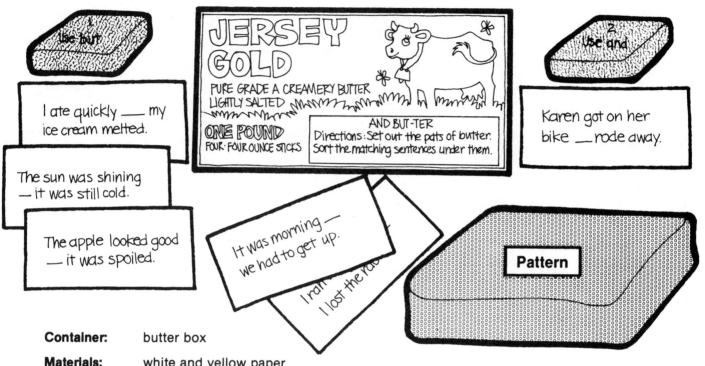

Container: butter box

Materials: white and yellow paper

Preparation:
1. Using the pattern, cut out two yellow pats of butter. Then, cut out sixteen strips of white paper, each measuring two inches by five inches.

2. On one pat write **Use but**, and on the other write **Use and**. Number these **1** and **2**.

3. On each strip write a sentence using **but** or **and**, omitting these words.
   Suggested sentence list:

   I ran fast, but I lost the race.
   I ate quickly, but my ice cream melted.
   Mary hurt her arm, but she did not cry.
   It rained, but my umbrella kept me dry.
   It did not snow, but I went sledding anyway.
   Mike made a good cake, but mine was better.
   The sun was shining, but it was still cold.
   The apple looked good, but it was spoiled.
   Bill went to the store and bought a cake.
   Mother sewed a dress, and it looked beautiful.
   It was morning, and we had to get up.
   Karen got on her bike and rode away.
   He always brushes his teeth and combs his hair.
   They sang a song and danced around.
   Jim screamed and ran around the room.
   He started his car and drove down the street.

4. For self-checking, number the backs of each sentence to match the pats of butter.

Directions: Set out the pats of butter. Sort the matching sentences under them.

Can You Top This?

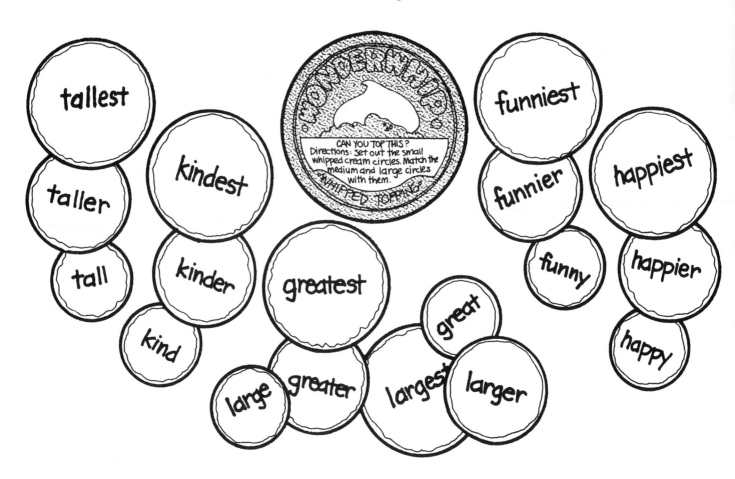

Container: whipped topping carton

Material: white paper

Preparation:

1. Cut out thirty circles: ten two inches in diameter, ten three inches in diameter, and ten four inches in diameter.

2. On the small circles write an adjective; on the medium circles, the comparative form of that adjective; and on the large circles, the superlative form of that adjective.

   Suggested word list:

funny, funnier, funniest	*large, larger, largest*
good, better, best	*less, lesser, least*
great, greater, greatest	*small, smaller, smallest*
happy, happier, happiest	*tall, taller, tallest*
kind, kinder, kindest	*tiny, tinier, tiniest*

3. For self-checking, number the backs of matching sets.

Directions: Set out the small whipped topping circles. Match the medium and large circles with them.

Popping Plurals

Container:	popcorn jar or can
Materials:	white and brown paper
Preparation:	1. Using the pattern, cut out fifteen white and three brown popcorn shapes.
	2. On one brown popcorn shape write **Add es**, on the second write **Add s**, and on the third write **Take away the y and add ies**. Number these **1**, **2**, and **3**.
	3. On the white popcorn shapes write words that fit these categories.

Suggested word list:

box	dog	baby
bus	duck	bunny
bush	house	candy
fox	rabbit	cherry
grass	tree	family

4. For self-checking, number the backs of the white popcorn shapes to match the brown popcorn shapes.

Directions: Set out the brown caramel corn. Sort the matching white popcorn under it.

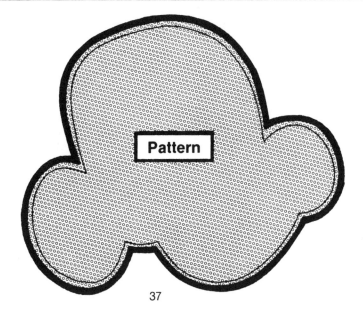

Pattern

Precious Plurals

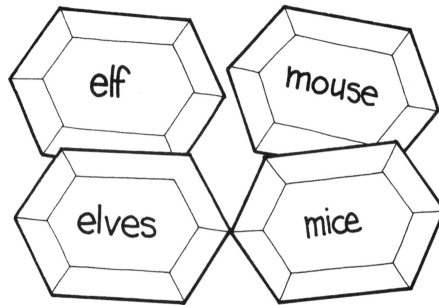

Container:	jewelry box
Materials:	white and red paper
Preparation:	1. Using the pattern, cut out fifteen red and fifteen white gem shapes.
	2. On the red gems write singular forms of nouns that have irregular plurals.
	3. On the white gems write their plural forms.

Suggested word list:

fish, fish	*calf, calves*	*life, lives*
sheep, sheep	*elf, elves*	*loaf, loaves*
man, men	*half, halves*	*self, selves*
mouse, mice	*knife, knives*	*shelf, shelves*
woman, women	*leaf, leaves*	*wolf, wolves*

4. For self-checking, number the backs of matching sets.

Directions: Line up the red gems. Sort the matching white gems under them.

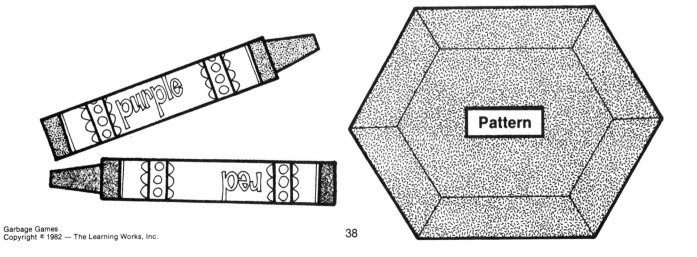

Nailing Down Opposites

Container:	nail box
Materials:	gray or white paper
Preparation:	1. Using the patterns, cut out two hammers and twenty nails.
	2. On one hammer write **Same**, and on the other write **Opposite**. Number these **1** and **2**.
	3. On ten of the nails write pairs of words that are opposites, and on the other ten write pairs of words that mean the same.

Suggested word list:

asleep, awake	happy, sad	big, large	grin, smile
big, little	short, tall	easy, simple	jump, leap
cold, hot	small, large	fat, plump	talk, speak
front, back	some, none	father, dad	thin, skinny
early, late	stop, go	glow, shine	tiny, little

4. For self-checking, number the backs of the nails to match the hammers.

Directions: Set out the hammers. Sort the matching nails under them.

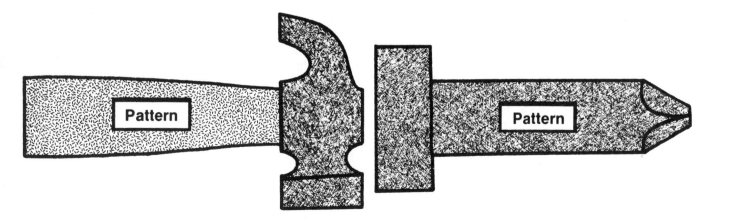

Cool Quiz

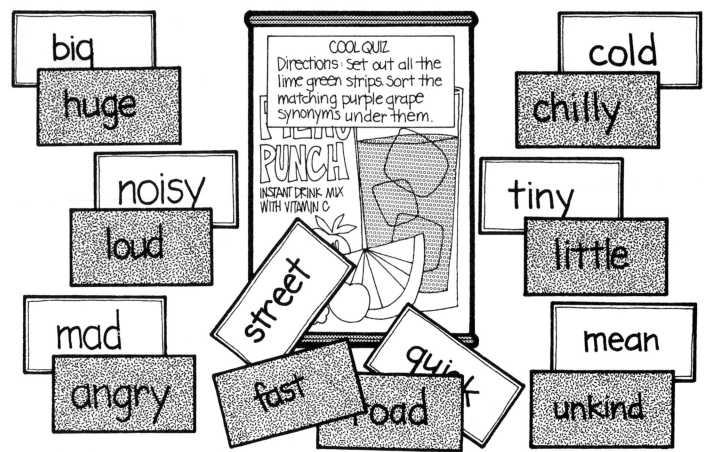

Container:	powdered fruit drink mix can
Materials:	green and purple paper
Preparation:	1. Cut ten purple and ten green strips of paper, each measuring one and one-half inches by three inches.
	2. Write words on the green strips and their synonyms on the purple.

Suggested word list:

beautiful, pretty	loud, noisy
big, huge	mad, angry
bold, brave	mean, unkind
close, near	shiny, bright
cool, chilly	sick, ill
dull, blunt	short, brief
fast, quick	street, road
happy, glad	shy, bashful
hard, difficult	thin, skinny
little, tiny	wealthy, rich

3. For self-checking, number the backs of matching sets.

Directions: Set out all the lime green strips. Sort the matching purple grape synonyms under them.

Cupcake Couples

Container: cupcake paper box

Materials: yellow and brown paper

Preparation:
1. Using the pattern, cut out twelve yellow and twelve brown cupcakes.
2. Write one word of a homonym pair on a yellow cupcake and the other word on a brown cupcake.

   Suggested word list:

ate, eight	*road, rode*
hear, here	*son, sun*
lie, lye	*through, threw*
new, knew	*to, two*
no, know	*weak, week*
red, read	*wood, would*

3. For self-checking, number the backs of matching sets.

Directions: Line up all the yellow cupcakes. Sort the matching brown cupcake homonyms under them.

Root It Out

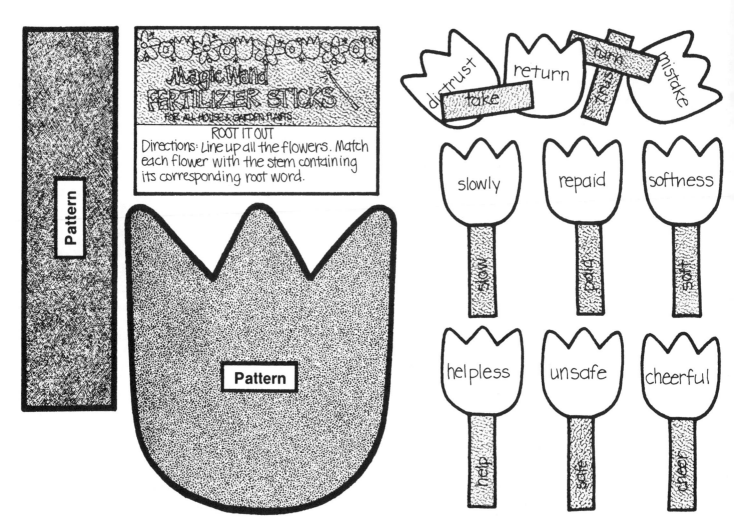

Magic Wand FERTILIZER STICKS
FOR ALL HOUSE & GARDEN PLANTS

ROOT IT OUT
Directions: Line up all the flowers. Match each flower with the stem containing its corresponding root word.

Container: any garden preparation box

Materials: paper in assorted colors (including green)

Preparation:
1. Using the patterns, cut out twenty flowers of assorted colors and twenty green stems.
2. Write words containing a prefix or suffix on each flower.
3. On the stems write their root words.

   Suggested word list:

brave, bravely	fair, unfair	paid, repaid	take, mistake
bright, brightness	glad, gladly	sad, sadness	thought, thoughtful
cheer, cheerful	help, helpless	safe, unsafe	true, untrue
cover, uncover	hope, hopeless	slow, slowly	trust, distrust
do, redo	new, renew	soft, softness	turn, return

4. For self-checking, number the backs of matching sets.

Directions: Line up all the flowers. Match each flower with the stem containing its corresponding root word.

Match-Up Muffins

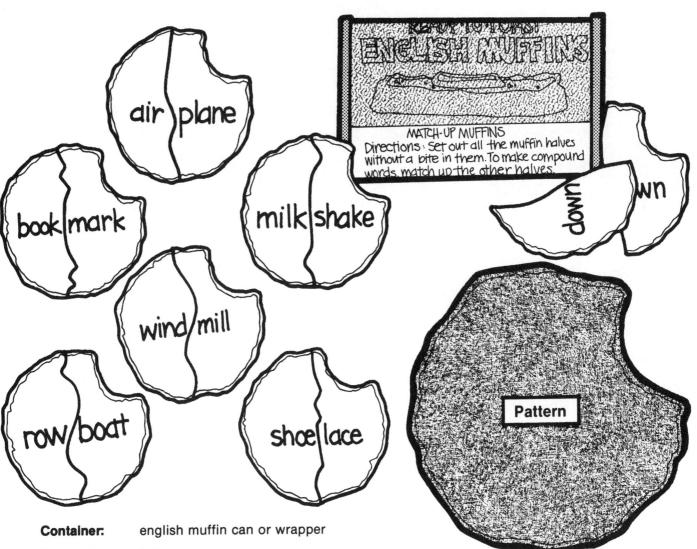

Container: english muffin can or wrapper

Material: light brown paper

Preparation: 1. Using the pattern, cut out twenty muffin shapes.

2. Write one compound word on each shape, putting the first part of the word on the part of the muffin without the bite in it.

3. Cut each muffin in half, dividing the compound word.

   Suggested word list:

airplane	daytime	homework	rainbow
basketball	downtown	horseshoe	rowboat
birthmark	drumstick	meatball	shoelace
bookmark	grasshopper	milkshake	sunlight
classroom	headband	newspaper	windmill

4. For self-checking, number the backs of matching sets.

Directions: Set out all the muffin halves without a bite in them. To make compound words, match up the other halves.

Perfect Pancake Prefixes

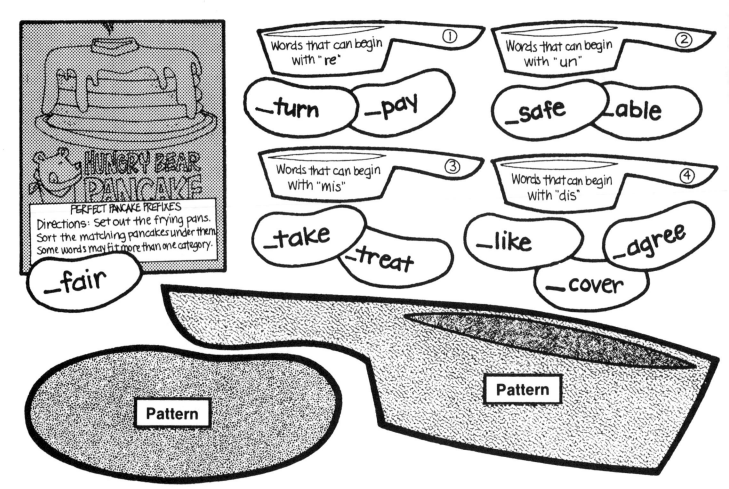

① Words that can begin with "re"	② Words that can begin with "un"
_turn _pay	_safe _able
③ Words that can begin with "mis"	④ Words that can begin with "dis"
_take _treat	_like _agree _cover

PERFECT PANCAKE PREFIXES

Directions: Set out the frying pans. Sort the matching pancakes under them. Some words may fit more than one category.

_fair

Pattern

Pattern

Container: pancake-mix box

Materials: yellow and gray paper

Preparation:
1. Using the patterns, cut out four gray frying pans and sixteen yellow pancakes.
2. On each frying pan write one of the following: **Words that can begin with re**, **Words that can begin with un**, **Words that can begin with mis**, or **Words that can begin with dis**. Number these **1** through **4**.
3. On each pancake, write a word that begins with **re**, **un**, **dis**, or **mis**, omitting these letters.

   Suggested word list:

disagree	mislead	rematch	unable
discover	misplace	renew	unfair
dislike	mistake	return	unsafe
dismiss	mistreat	rewrite	untrue

4. For self-checking, number the backs of the pancakes to match the frying pans. (Some words may fit more than one category.)

Directions: Set out the frying pans. Sort the matching pancakes under them.
Some words may fit more than one category.

Snappy Suffixes

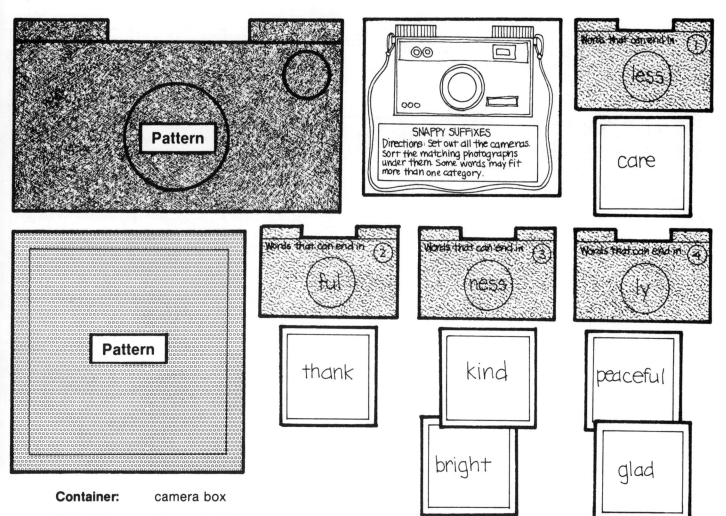

Container: camera box

Materials: blue and white paper

Preparation:

1. Using the patterns, cut out and mark four blue cameras and twenty white photographs.

2. On each camera write one of the following: **Words that can end in less, Words that can end in ful, Words that can end in ness,** or **Words that can end in ly.** Number these **1** through **4.**

3. On each photograph write a word that could end in **less**, **ful**, **ness**, or **ly**.
   Suggested word list:

bad	*dark*	*hope*	*peace*	*slow*
bright	*glad*	*joy*	*quick*	*thank*
care	*harm*	*kind*	*sad*	*thought*
cheer	*help*	*light*	*shame*	*use*

4. For self-checking, number the backs of the photographs to match the cameras.

Directions: Set out the cameras. Sort the matching photographs under them.

Shredded Words

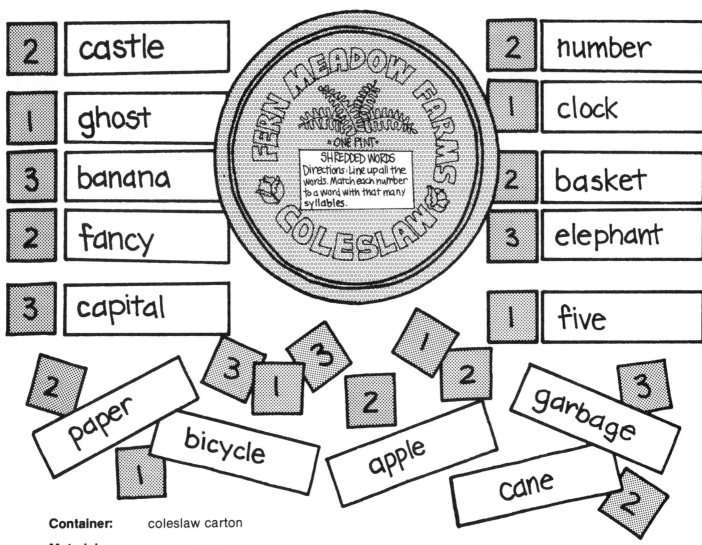

Container: coleslaw carton

Material: green paper

Preparation:
1. Cut fifteen strips of green paper one inch by four inches each, and fifteen one-inch squares.
2. On the strips write words with a varying number of syllables, and on the squares write the number of syllables in each.

   Suggested word list:

cane	basket	paper
clock	castle	banana
five	fancy	bicycle
ghost	garbage	capital
apple	number	elephant

3. For self-checking, write the correct number of syllables on the back of each word strip.

Directions: Line up all the words. Match a number to a word with that many syllables.

Add an Accent

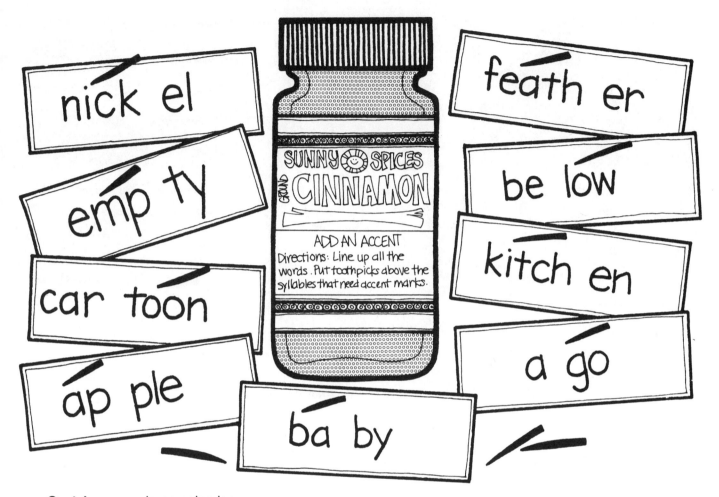

Container: large spice jar

Materials: white paper and five colored toothpicks

Preparation:
1. Cut twenty strips of paper one and one-half inches by three and one-half inches each.
2. On each strip write a word broken into syllables.
3. Cut toothpicks in four even pieces for use as accent marks.

   Suggested word list:

a bout'	be low'	emp' ty	moth' er
ac' tion	ca noe'	ev' er y	nick' el
a go'	car toon'	feath' er	o' ver
ap' ple	dress' er	ghost' ly	pic' ture
ba' by	dust' y	kitch' en	with out'

4. For self-checking, rewrite the word on the back of each strip and indicate the accented syllable.

Directions: Line up all the words. Put toothpicks above the syllables that need accent marks.

Peanut Possessives

Container:	peanut butter jar
Materials:	light and dark brown paper
Preparation:	1. Using the pattern, cut out nine light brown and nine dark brown peanuts.
	2. On the light brown peanuts write possessive nouns or pronouns.
	3. On the dark brown peanuts write their meanings.

Suggested word list:

the cat's - belonging to the cat	his - belonging to him
the man's - belonging to the man	hers - belonging to her
Mary's - belonging to Mary	its - belonging to it
mine - belonging to me	theirs - belonging to them
ours - belonging to us	

4. For self-checking, put the same number on the back of each matched possessive noun or pronoun and its meaning.

Directions: Line up the light brown peanuts. Match up the dark brown peanuts with them.

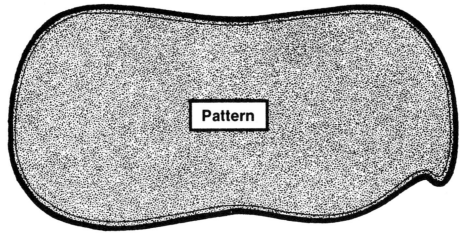

Who Wants What Wonderful Waffles?

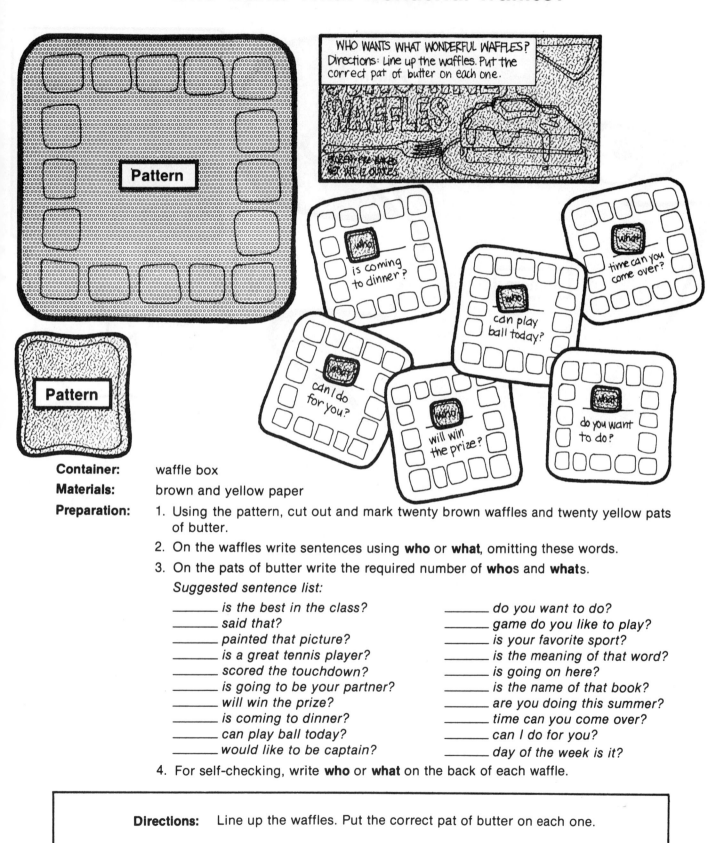

Container:	waffle box
Materials:	brown and yellow paper
Preparation:	

1. Using the pattern, cut out and mark twenty brown waffles and twenty yellow pats of butter.

2. On the waffles write sentences using **who** or **what**, omitting these words.

3. On the pats of butter write the required number of **who**s and **what**s.

   Suggested sentence list:

   _____ is the best in the class?   _____ do you want to do?
   _____ said that?   _____ game do you like to play?
   _____ painted that picture?   _____ is your favorite sport?
   _____ is a great tennis player?   _____ is the meaning of that word?
   _____ scored the touchdown?   _____ is going on here?
   _____ is going to be your partner?   _____ is the name of that book?
   _____ will win the prize?   _____ are you doing this summer?
   _____ is coming to dinner?   _____ time can you come over?
   _____ can play ball today?   _____ can I do for you?
   _____ would like to be captain?   _____ day of the week is it?

4. For self-checking, write **who** or **what** on the back of each waffle.

Directions: Line up the waffles. Put the correct pat of butter on each one.

Fishing for Meaning

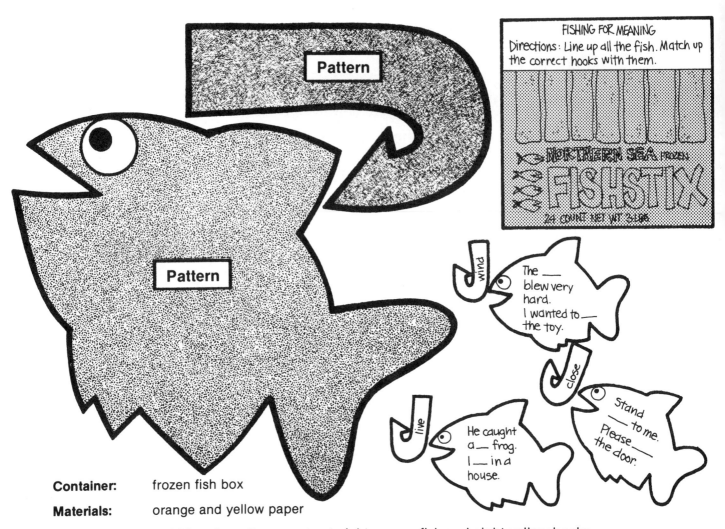

Container: frozen fish box

Materials: orange and yellow paper

Preparation:
1. Using the patterns, cut out eight orange fish and eight yellow hooks.
2. On each hook write a homograph (multiple-meaning word).
3. On each fish write two sentences that indicate the different meanings and pronunciations for these words.

   Suggested word and sentence list:

bass	A _____ is a kind of fish. He played the _____ drum.
bow	She will _____ before the queen. Mary wore a _____ in her hair.
close	Stand _____ to me. Please _____ the door.
live	He caught a _____ frog. I _____ in a house.
read	I will _____ the book. I _____ the story yesterday.
sow	Another name for a pig is a _____ . I will _____ the seeds.
tear	A _____ ran down her cheek. My shirt has a _____ in it.
wind	The _____ blew very hard. I wanted to _____ the toy.

4. For self-checking, put the same number on the back of each matched fish and hook.

Directions: Line up all the fish. Match up the correct hooks with them.

Curling Commas

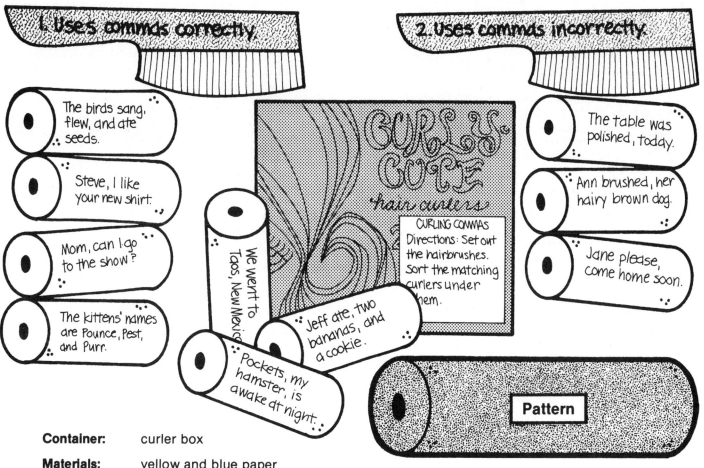

Container: curler box

Materials: yellow and blue paper

Preparation:
1. Using the patterns, cut out two blue hairbrushes and twenty yellow curlers.
2. On one hairbrush write **Uses commas correctly**, and on the other write **Uses commas incorrectly**. Number these **1** and **2**.
3. On each of ten curlers write a sentence in which commas are used correctly, and on each of the other ten curlers write a sentence in which commas are used incorrectly. (Use sentences at the appropriate reading level.)
4. For self-checking, number the backs of the curlers to match the hairbrushes.

Directions: Set out the hairbrushes. Sort the matching curlers under them.

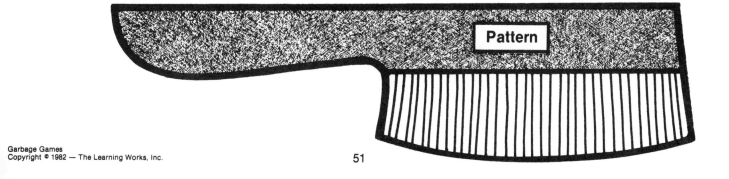

Large Letters

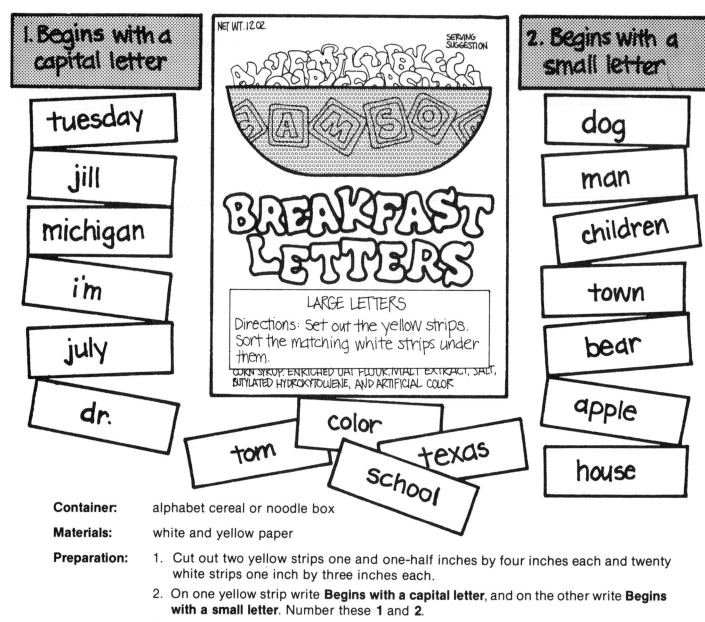

1. Begins with a capital letter		2. Begins with a small letter
tuesday		dog
jill		man
michigan		children
i'm		town
july		bear
dr.		apple
		house

NET WT. 12 OZ.   SERVING SUGGESTION

BREAKFAST LETTERS

LARGE LETTERS
Directions: Set out the yellow strips. Sort the matching white strips under them.

CORN SYRUP, ENRICHED OAT FLOUR, MALT EXTRACT, SALT, BUTYLATED HYDROXYTOLUENE, AND ARTIFICIAL COLOR

color   tom   texas   school

Container: alphabet cereal or noodle box

Materials: white and yellow paper

Preparation: 1. Cut out two yellow strips one and one-half inches by four inches each and twenty white strips one inch by three inches each.

2. On one yellow strip write **Begins with a capital letter**, and on the other write **Begins with a small letter**. Number these **1** and **2**.

3. On each of the white strips, write (in lowercase) some words that should be capitalized and some that should remain lowercase.

Suggested word list:

apple	color	school	i'm	st.
baby	dog	town	jill	texas
bear	house	america	july	tom
children	man	dr.	michigan	tuesday

4. For self-checking, number the backs of the white strips to match the yellow ones.

Directions: Set out the yellow strips. Sort the matching white strips under them.

Salad Sentences

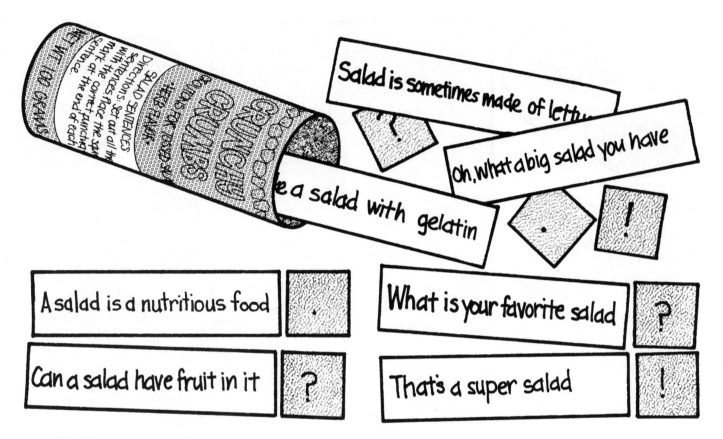

Container:	crouton can
Material:	green paper
Preparation:	1. Cut ten strips of green paper, each measuring one and one-half inches by six inches, and ten one and one-half inch squares.

2. Write a sentence about salads on each strip and write the ending punctuation mark for that sentence on a square.

   Suggested sentence list:

   Salad is a nutritious food.
   Salad is sometimes made with lettuce.
   A salad made with cabbage is called coleslaw.
   I know of a salad called George Washington.
   What is your favorite salad?
   Can you make a salad with gelatin?
   Can a salad have fruit in it?
   Oh, what a big salad you have!
   That's a super salad!
   Gee, that's a tiny head of lettuce!

3. For self-checking, write the correct punctuation mark on the back of each strip.

Directions: Set out all the sentences. Place the square with the correct punctuation mark at the end of each sentence.

Cookie Contractions

Container: cookie box or tin

Materials: pink and brown paper

Preparation:
1. Cut out ten pink and ten brown circles, each measuring three inches in diameter.
2. Write contractions on the brown circles.
3. Write the two words in each contraction on the pink circles.

   Suggested word list:

I'm, I am	*I'll, I will*
we're, we are	*we'll, we will*
he's, he is	*he'll, he will*
she's, she is	*she'll, she will*
they're, they are	*they'll, they will*

4. For self-checking, write the same number on the back of the brown circle and the pink circle in each matched set.

Directions: Line up the brown cookies. Match the pink cookies with them.

Quick Quotes

Container:	quick-cooking oatmeal box
Materials:	white paper and clear plastic bingo disks

Preparation:

1. Cut ten strips of paper, each measuring one and one-half inches by eight inches.

2. On each strip write a sentence in which quotation marks are needed. Include all other necessary punctuation but omit the quotation marks.

3. Break each sentence into quotational parts with diagonal lines.

   Suggested sentence list:

   Come home early, / said mother.
   Oh, / said Jan, / it's just perfect.
   Bill said, / That's a good job!
   What do you want to do? / asked Dad.
   I like math, / said Fred.
   My sister is coming, too, / called Mark.
   Why is the house dark? / asked Alan.
   It's time to cut the grass, / said Grandma.
   Can you play today? / asked Karen.
   Yes, / said his teacher, / you're right.

4. For self-checking, put a dot on the back of each strip to indicate the part(s) that need(s) quotation marks.

Directions: Line up all the sentences. Place disks on those parts in each sentence that need quotation marks.

Brushing up on Abbeviations

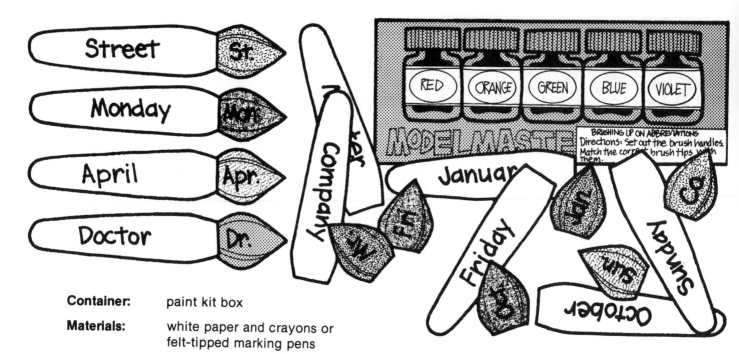

Container: paint kit box

Materials: white paper and crayons or felt-tipped marking pens

Preparation:

1. Using the patterns, cut out twenty brush handles and brush tips.

2. Color the brush tips various colors.

3. On the brush tips write abbreviations, and on the brush handles write the words they stand for.

    Suggested word list:

Avenue, Ave.	Sunday, Sun.	January, Jan.	November, Nov.
Company, Co.	Monday, Mon.	February, Feb.	December, Dec.
Doctor, Dr.	Tuesday, Tues.	March, Mar.	
Mister, Mr.	Wednesday, Wed.	April, Apr.	
Mistress, Mrs.	Thursday, Thurs.	August, Aug.	
Road, Rd.	Saturday, Sat.	October, Oct.	

4. For self-checking, write the same number on the back of the brush handle and tip in each matched set.

Directions: Set out the brush handles. Match the correct brush tips with them.

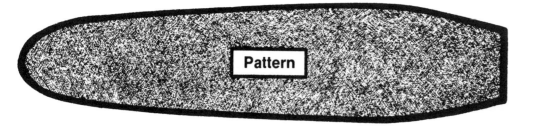

Pattern

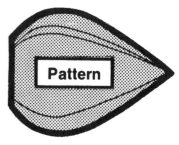

Pattern

Socks Box

Container: sock or hose box

Materials: green and white paper

Preparation:
1. Using the patterns, cut out two green socks and twenty white darning needles.
2. On one sock write **Words beginning with sc**, and on the other write **Words beginning with sk**. Number these **1** and **2**.
3. On the needles write words that begin with **sc** or **sk**, omitting these letters.

Suggested word list:

scab	school	scratch	skid	skit
scale	scoop	scream	skin	skull
scare	scout	skate	skip	skunk
scat	scrap	ski	skirt	sky

4. For self-checking, number the backs of the needles to match the socks.

Directions: Set out the socks. Sort the matching darning needles under them.

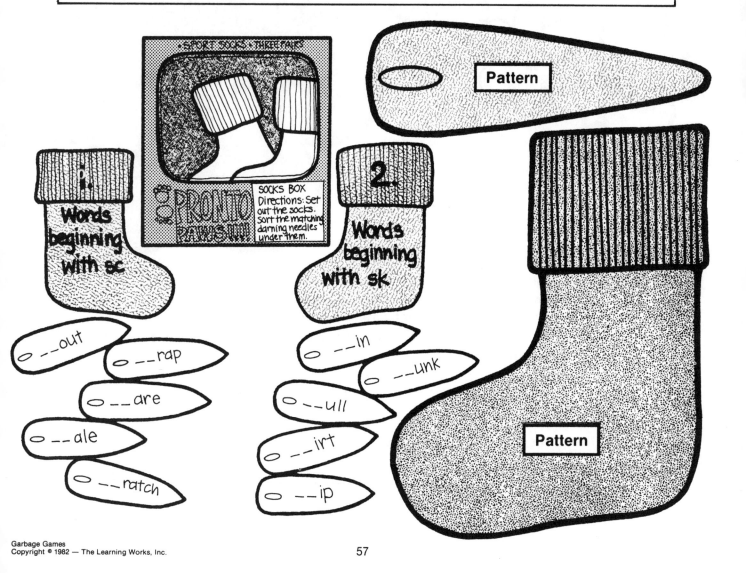

Flour Power

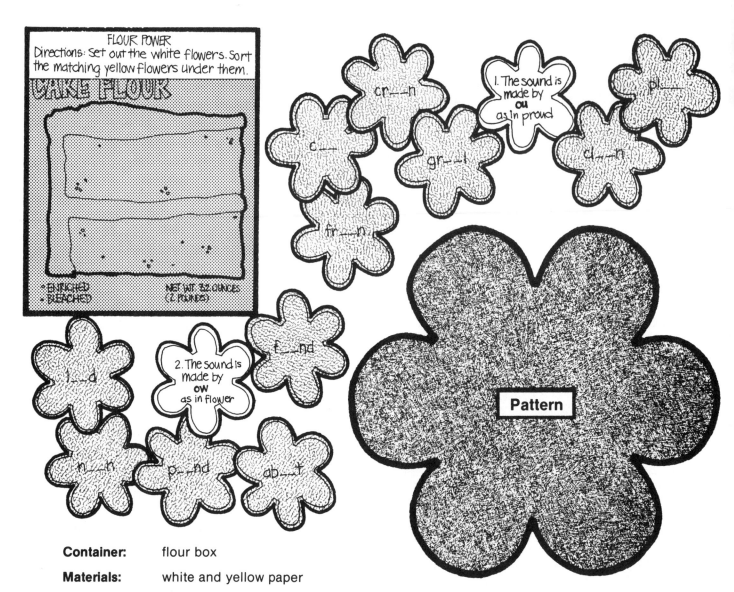

Container: flour box

Materials: white and yellow paper

Preparation:
1. Using the pattern, cut out two white and twenty yellow flowers.
2. On one white flower write **The sound is made by ou as in proud**, and on the other write **The sound is made by ow as in flower**. Number these **1** and **2**.
3. On the yellow flowers write words that contain **ou** or **ow**, omitting these letters.

   Suggested word list:

about	loud	round	crowd	now
cloud	noun	sound	crown	plow
found	pound	cow	frown	power
ground	proud	clown	growl	shower

4. For self-checking, number the backs of the yellow flowers to match the white ones.

Directions: Set out the white flowers. Sort the matching yellow flowers under them.

Right Writer

Container: envelope box

Materials: blue and yellow paper

Preparation:
1. Using the patterns, cut out two blue ink bottles and twenty yellow pens.
2. On one bottle write **Spelled with r**, and on the other write **Spelled with wr**. Number these **1** and **2**.
3. On the pens write words that begin with **r** and **wr**, omitting these letters in each word.

   Suggested word list:

race	rest	rope	wreath	wrist
ran	ride	running	wreck	write
reach	ripe	wrangle	wrestle	wrong
real	rooster	wrapper	wrinkle	wrote

4. For self-checking, number the backs of the pens to match the ink bottles.

Directions: Set out the ink bottles. Sort the matching pens under them.

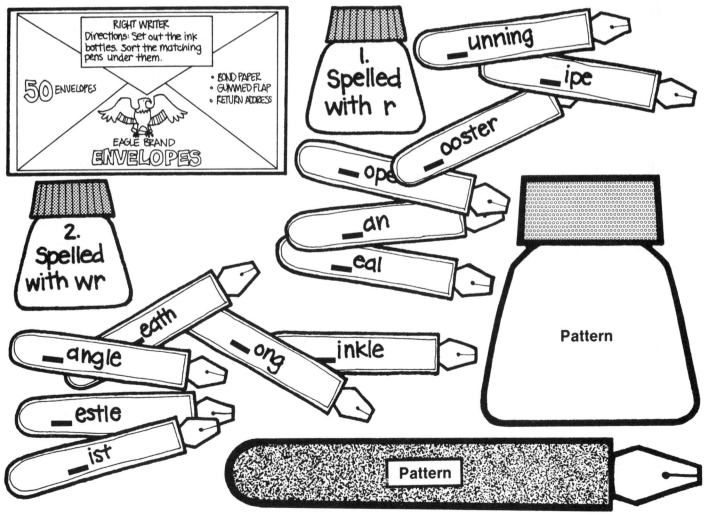

Bird Words

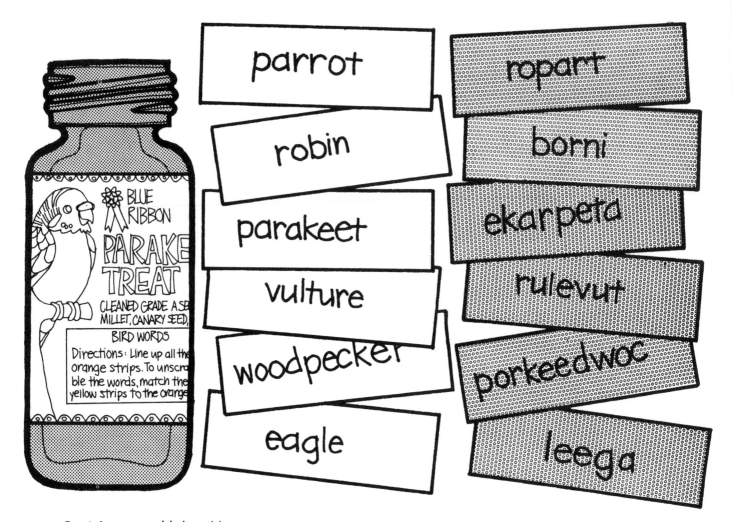

parrot	ropart
robin	borni
parakeet	ekanpeta
vulture	rulevut
woodpecker	porkeedwoc
eagle	leega

Container: birdseed jar

Materials: yellow and orange paper

Preparation:
1. Cut ten yellow strips and ten orange strips, each measuring one inch by three inches.
2. Write bird names on the yellow strips and scrambled versions of the same names on the orange strips.

   Suggested word list:

bluejay	*robin*
canary	*sparrow*
eagle	*vulture*
parakeet	*woodpecker*
parrot	*wren*

3. For self-checking, put the same number on the back of each strip in a matched pair.

Directions: Line up all the orange strips. To unscramble the words, match the yellow strips to the orange ones.

Margarine Mix-Ups

Container: margarine tub

Materials: pale yellow paper and dark yellow paper

Preparation:
1. Using the pattern, cut out ten pale yellow pats of margarine and ten dark yellow ones.
2. Write the names of foods eaten with margarine on the pale yellow pats and scrambled versions of these names on the dark yellow pats.

   Suggested word list:

bun	potato
bread	roll
corn	sandwich
muffin	toast
popcorn	waffle

3. For self-checking, put the same number on the back of each pat in a matched pair.

Directions: Line up all of the dark yellow margarine pats. To unscramble the words, match the pale yellow pats to the dark yellow ones.

Better Letter

CIRCUS STATIONERY

12 DECORATED SHEETS • 12 PLAIN SHEETS • 12 ENVELOPES

BETTER LETTER
Directions: Set out the letter. Line up the yellow strips to match their order in the letter.

① Jan Brown
6436 Orange St.
Ojai, Calif. 93023

② Dear Mark,

Thank you so much for coming to visit me. I really enjoyed having you here.

Going to the zoo was fun. My favorite animal was the elephant. Which one did you like best? ③

I hope you can come again soon.

Have a good summer.

④ Your friend,
⑤ Jan

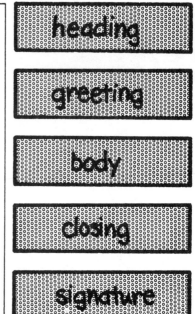

heading

greeting

body

closing

signature

Container:	stationery box
Materials:	yellow paper and a sheet of stationery
Preparation:	

1. On the stationery, write a letter and number its major parts (heading, greeting, body, closing, and signature).
2. Cut five strips of yellow paper, each measuring one inch by four inches.
3. On each strip write one of the following: **Heading, Greeting, Body, Closing,** or **Signature**.

Suggested letter:

Jan Brown
6436 Orange St.
Ojai, Calif. 93023

Dear Mark,

    Thank you so much for coming to visit me. I really enjoyed having you here.
    Going to the zoo was fun. My favorite animal was the elephant. Which one did you like best?
    I hope you can come again soon. Have a good summer.

          Your friend,
          Jan

4. For self-checking, number the backs of the yellow strips to match the numbers on the letter.

Directions: Set out the letter. Line up the yellow strips to match their order in the letter.

Mirror Madness

Container: mirror box

Material: white paper

Preparation: 1. Cut out two mirrors, using the pattern, and twenty strips of paper one and one-half inches by four inches each.

2. On one mirror write **Positive Statements**, and on the other write **Matching Negative Statements**. Number these **1** and **2**.

3. On each of ten strips write positive statements, and on each of the other ten strips write the matching negative statements.

Suggested statement list:

The flowers grow very well. — The flowers do not grow very well.
The children like to play outdoors. — The children do not like to play outdoors.
Apples are my favorite fruit. — Apples are not my favorite fruit.
Baking cakes is fun. — Baking cakes is not fun.
A large tree grew in the yard. — A large tree did not grow in the yard.
The ice cream came in many flavors. — The ice cream did not come in many flavors.
Our fire is burning brightly. — Our fire is not burning brightly.
We like to swim on hot days. — We do not like to swim on hot days.
Their baskets were filled with fruit. — Their baskets were not filled with fruit.
The brown dog barked at the girl. — The brown dog did not bark at the girl.

4. For self-checking, number the backs of matching sets.

Directions: Set out the mirrors. Match the sentence strips with them.

Pattern

The flowers grow very well.	The flowers do not grow very well.
Apples are my favorite fruit.	Apples are not my favorite fruit.
Baking cakes is fun.	Baking cakes is not fun.
Our fire is burning brightly.	Our fire is not burning brightly.

Sweet and Salty Samples

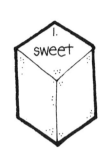

SWEET AND SALTY SAMPLES
Directions: Set out the white sugar cube and salt shaker. Sort the yellow food strips under them.

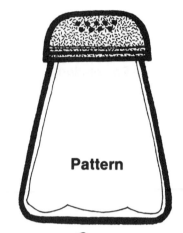

Pattern

cookies
syrup
cherries
ice cream
jelly beans
strawberries

peanuts

honey

popcorn
potato chips
crackers
corn chips
pretzels
French fries

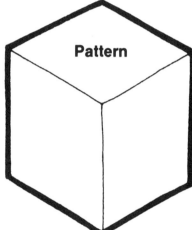

Pattern

Container: salt box

Materials: white and yellow paper

Preparation:
1. Using the patterns, cut out a white sugar cube and a white salt shaker.
2. Cut sixteen yellow strips of paper, each measuring one inch by four inches.
3. On the sugar cube write **Sweet**, and on the salt shaker write **Salty**. Number these **1** and **2**.
4. Write the names of foods that are sweet or salty on the yellow strips.

   Suggested food list:

cherries	*corn chips*
cookies	*crackers*
honey	*french fries*
ice cream	*peanuts*
jelly beans	*popcorn*
marshmallows	*potato chips*
strawberries	*pretzels*
syrup	*tortilla chips*

5. For self-checking, number the backs of the strips to match the sugar cube or the salt shaker.

Directions: Set out the white sugar cube and salt shaker. Sort the yellow food strips under them.

LANGUAGE
DESCRIPTIVE WORDS

Fruitful Facts

Container: fruit-flavored cereal box

Materials: stiff white paper, scissors, white glue, and pictures of the following fruits: apple, banana, cherries, grapes, lemon, orange, peach, pineapple, plum, strawberry

Preparation:
1. From stiff white paper, cut ten cards, each measuring three inches by five inches.
2. Draw or glue the picture of one fruit on each card.
3. Cut twenty strips of paper, each measuring one inch by five inches.
4. Write a descriptive word for fruit on each of these strips.

Suggested word list:

bumpy	hard	red	soft
crisp	juicy	round	sour
fuzzy	orange	shiny	spiny
green	pink	small	sweet
yellow	purple	smooth	tart

5. Allow children to be creative in matching descriptive words with fruits. If matches seem unusual or inappropriate, encourage them to explain—and enjoy their explanations.

Directions: Set out the fruit cards. Sort the descriptive words under them. Be creative in your combinations. Some words may go with more than one fruit.

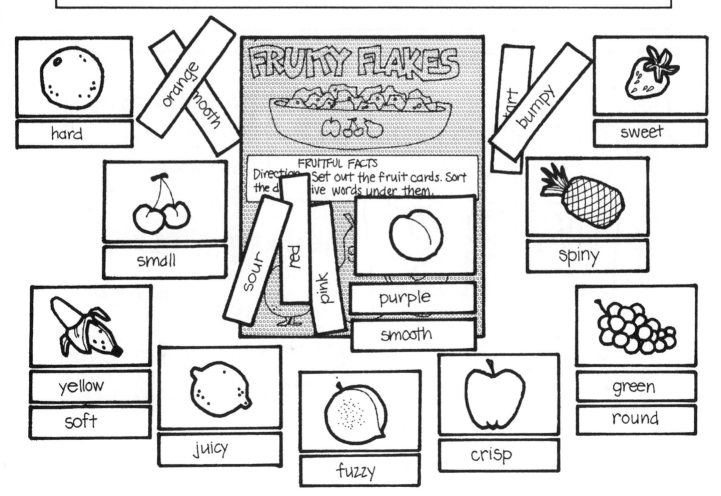

Squeezing out the Right Order

Container: sponge bag

Materials: yellow, white, and blue paper

Preparation:

1. Cut six two-inch-by-six-inch strips each of yellow, white, and blue paper.

2. Write three short paragraphs. Using a different color of paper for each paragraph, write one sentence of the paragraph on each strip.

    Suggested paragraphs:

    Mary woke up early in the morning. She climbed out of bed. She got dressed. She ate breakfast. She packed her lunch. It was time to leave for school.

    Bob put on his uniform. He walked quickly to the ball park. He saw the men getting the field ready. It was time to play ball. The umpire called Bob safe. He had helped to win the game.

    The bell rang for lunch. The children lined up. They sat down at the long tables. Bill opened his lunch box. He saw that his mother had packed fruit for him. This was going to be a good lunch.

3. For self-checking, number the backs of the strips in each set in sequential order.

Directions: Sort the sentences into three color piles. Put each set in the right story order.

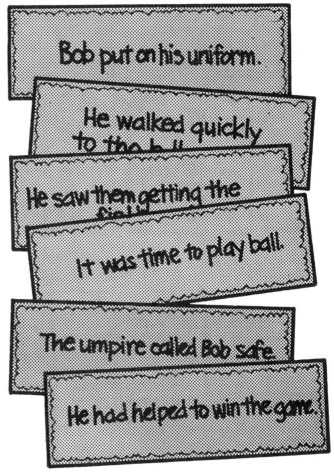

Pencil People

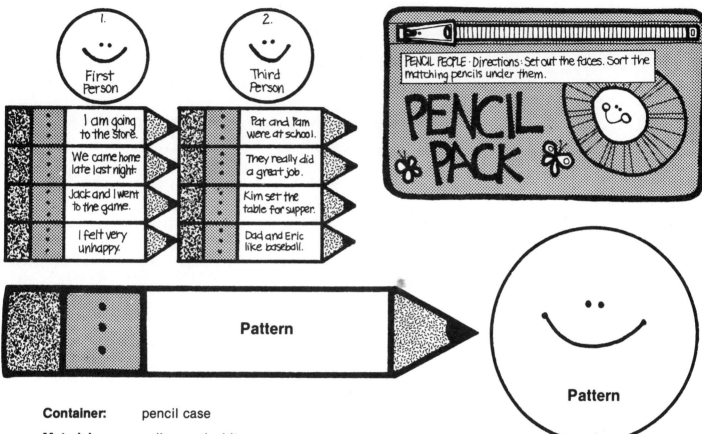

Container: pencil case

Materials: yellow and white paper

Preparation:

1. Using the patterns, cut out and mark two white faces and twenty yellow pencils.

2. On one face write **First Person**, and on the other write **Third Person**. Number these **1** and **2**.

3. On ten pencils write sentences in the first person, and on the other ten write sentences in the third person.

   Suggested sentence list:

I am going to the store.	*Pat and Pam were at school.*
You and I are good at skating.	*They really did a great job.*
Jack and I went to the game.	*Lee started to cut the lawn.*
I felt very unhappy.	*Jim's table won first prize.*
It was my turn to be first.	*Kim set the table for supper.*
My uncle likes to ski.	*Dave and Kurt rode their bikes.*
Karen, Mike, and I are friends.	*Mother picked the beautiful flowers.*
My picture was the best in the class.	*Dad and Eric like baseball.*
John liked my new shirt.	*The rain ruined their picnic.*
We came home late last night.	*It was the best trip they ever took.*

4. For self-checking, number the backs of the pencils to match the faces.

Directions: Set out the faces. Sort the matching pencils under them.

Light Lovely Language

Container: light bulb box

Materials: white and yellow paper

Preparation:
1. Using the pattern, cut out two yellow and twenty white light bulbs.
2. On one yellow bulb write **Simile**, and on the other write **Metaphor**. Number these **1** and **2**.
3. On ten of the white bulbs write similes, and on the other ten write metaphors.
   Suggested list:

   Similes
   The tree was like a giant.
   Mary was like a ghost.
   He was as cold as ice.
   Stars glistened like diamonds.
   Greta is like an angel.
   The night was like a black cat.
   Our brother ran like lightning.
   The house was like a box.
   The raindrops were like large tears.
   The clouds looked like giant marshmallows.

   Metaphors
   The moon is a big yellow ball.
   My dress is a dream.
   Mark is a little devil.
   Josh is a walking dictionary.
   A kitten is a furry ball.
   My bike is a rocket.
   His pillow is a cloud.
   The fog is a blanket.
   From high above, all the people were ants
   Her eyes were black marbles.
4. For self-checking, number the white light bulbs to match the yellow ones.

> **Directions:**   Set out the yellow bulbs. Sort the matching white bulbs under them.

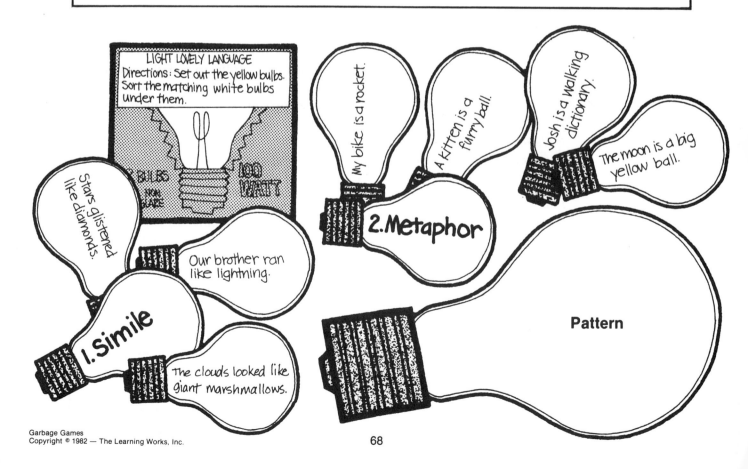

Figuring on Your Fingers

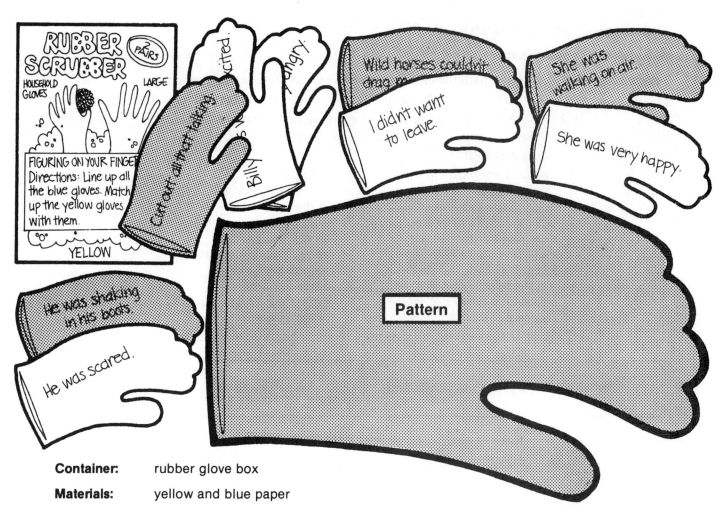

RUBBER SCRUBBER PAIRS
HOUSEHOLD GLOVES LARGE

FIGURING ON YOUR FINGER
Directions: Line up all
the blue gloves. Match
up the yellow gloves
with them.
YELLOW

Cut out all that talking.

Billy was just flying.

He was shaking in his boots.

He was scared.

Wild horses couldn't drag me away.

I didn't want to leave.

She was walking on air.

She was very happy.

Pattern

Container:	rubber glove box
Materials:	yellow and blue paper

Preparation:

1. Using the pattern, cut out ten blue and ten yellow gloves.

2. On the ten blue gloves write figures of speech, and on the yellow gloves write their meanings.

   Suggested list:

   Billy is number one with me. — Billy is a terrific boy.
   He blew his top. — He became very angry and shouted.
   She was walking on air. — She was very happy.
   Mary was mad as a wet hen. — Mary was very angry.
   Don't hold your breath. — Don't count on it to happen soon.
   Cut out all that talking. — Stop all the talking.
   Wild horses couldn't drag me away. — I didn't want to leave.
   Billy was just flying. — Billy was very excited.
   He was shaking in his boots. — He was scared.
   They spent the day chewing the fat. — They spent the day talking.

3. For self-checking, put the same number on the backs of each pair of matched gloves.

Directions: Line up all the blue gloves. Match up the yellow gloves with them.

A Place Setting

Container: plastic cutlery box

Material: yellow paper

Preparation:
1. Using the patterns, cut out two knives, ten forks, and ten spoons.
2. On one knife write **Time**, and on the other write **Place**. Number these **1** and **2**.
3. On the forks and spoons, write different times and places, alternating spoons and forks.

   Suggested list:

   early in the morning   at the old mill
   at high noon   in the living room
   during the evening   in the lake
   as the clock struck one   on top of the mountain
   on the Fourth of July   around the old barn
   after the show   above the little house
   before school   high in the sky
   in the middle of lunch   close to home
   as soon as they got there   across the bridge
   when her mother called her   near the farm

4. For self-checking, number the forks and spoons to match the knives.

Directions: Set out the knives. Sort the matching forks and spoons under them.

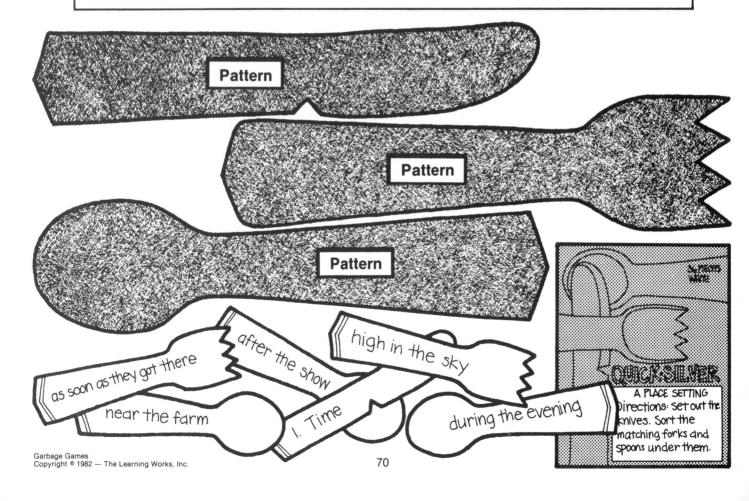

Rhyme Time

Container:	wristwatch box
Materials:	white and yellow paper
Preparation:	1. Using the patterns, cut out fifteen white clocks, fifteen small yellow hands, and fifteen large yellow hands.
	2. Write numbers on the faces of the clocks.
	3. On each small hand, write a word.
	4. On each large hand, write a word that rhymes with one of these words.

Suggested word list:

big, twig	*fan, pan*	*hot, spot*
boat, coat	*fast, last*	*mail, tale*
box, fox	*fry, cry*	*no, grow*
day, weigh	*hand, band*	*pin, grin*
eight, gate	*hen, ten*	*stone, bone*

5. For self-checking, put the same number on the back of the small hand and large hand in each rhymed pair.

Directions:	Line up all the clocks. Put a small hand on each. Then match a rhyming large hand with it.

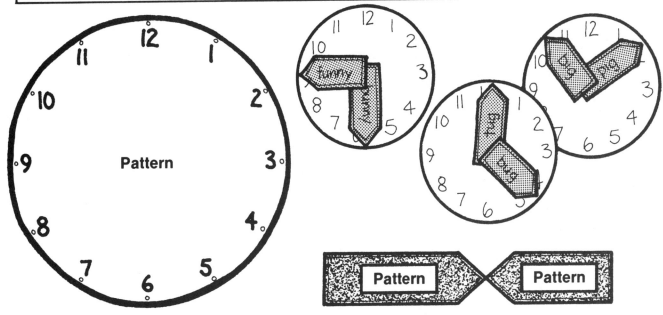

Cover Up

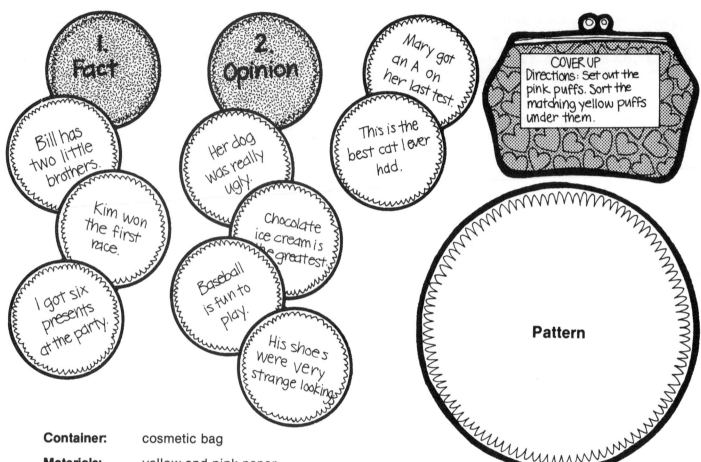

Container: cosmetic bag

Materials: yellow and pink paper

Preparation:
1. Using the pattern, cut out two pink and twenty yellow powder puffs.
2. On one pink puff write **Fact**, and on the other write **Opinion**. Number these **1** and **2**.
3. On ten yellow puffs write sentences that are factual, and on the other ten write sentences that are opinions.

Suggested sentence list:

Your new dress is beautiful.　　　　*Mary got an A on her last test.*
This is the best cat I ever had.　　　*Bill has two little brothers.*
Chocolate ice cream is the greatest.　*We lived in a white and green house.*
Baseball is fun to play.　　　　　　*Her eyes are blue.*
That chair is the softest.　　　　　*She was the second one to come home.*
It looked like the brightest star.　　*Kim won the first race.*
Her dog was really ugly.　　　　　　*The table was painted red.*
The fire was not very hot.　　　　　*There were two apples on the tree.*
John ran slowly down the street.　　*The stars are in the sky.*
His shoes were very strange looking.　*I got six presents at the party.*

4. For self-checking, number the backs of the yellow puffs to match the pink ones.

Directions: Set out the pink puffs. Sort the matching yellow puffs under them.

The Jig Is Up

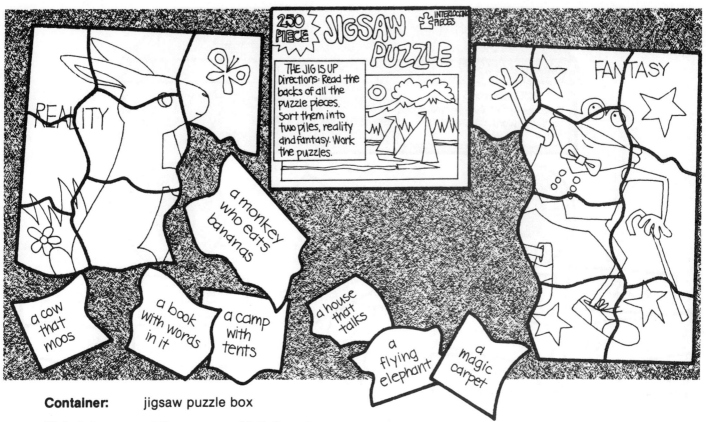

Container:	jigsaw puzzle box
Materials:	white paper and felt-tipped pens or crayons

Preparation:

1. Trace or draw two pictures on nine-by-twelve-inch sheets of white paper.
2. Color each picture.
3. Label one picture **Fantasy** and the other **Reality**.
4. Cut each picture into a jigsaw puzzle.
5. On the backs of the pieces of one puzzle, write realistic phrases; and on the backs of the pieces of the other puzzle, write fantastic phrases.

   Suggested phrase list:

a large cow with feathers	*an old woman rocking*
a flying elephant	*a mother who bakes*
a house that talks	*a cow that moos*
a tree that walks	*grass that grows green*
a six-eyed frog	*a boy who can sing*
a magic carpet	*a monkey who eats bananas*
a boy who grew to be twenty-five feet tall	*a camp with tents*
a car that drank milk	*a child who goes to school*
a giraffe who could play the piano	*a swimming pool with water*
a town that disappeared	*a book with words in it*

6. Self-checking is accomplished when the children successfully complete both puzzles.

Directions:	Read the backs of all the puzzle pieces. Sort them into two piles, reality and fantasy. Work the puzzles.

Rolling Along

Container: wax paper box

Materials: black, white, and gray paper

Preparation:
1. Cut out two gray circles two and three-fourths inches in diameter and two black circles one and one-fourth inches in diameter.

2. Cut fifteen strips of white paper, each measuring one inch by three inches.

3. Glue the black circles onto the gray circles to make wheels.

4. On one wheel write **Things with wheels**, and on the other write **Things without wheels**. Number these **1** and **2**.

5. On each of ten strips write an object that has wheels, and on each of five strips write an object that does not.

   Suggested word list:

bicycle	*tricycle*	*boat*
buggy	*truck*	*helicopter*
car	*unicycle*	*sled*
lawnmower	*wagon*	*sleigh*
train	*wheelbarrow*	*toboggan*

6. For self-checking, number the backs of the strips to match the wheels.

Directions: Set out the wheels. Sort the word strips under them.

Silver Lining

Container: aluminum foil box

Materials: white and gray or silver paper

Preparation:
1. Using the pattern, cut out two gray and twenty white clouds.
2. On one gray (silver) cloud write **Things that shine**, and on the other write **Things that don't shine**. Number these **1** and **2**.
3. On each of ten white clouds write an object that shines, and on each of ten others write an object that does not shine.

   Suggested word list:

diamond	light bulb	star	cement	rug
foil	mirror	sun	dirt	skin
glass	moon	brick	grass	tree
gold	silver	cardboard	hay	yarn

4. For self-checking, number the backs of the white clouds to match the gray ones.

Directions: Set out the gray clouds. Sort the white clouds under them.

Pattern

A Slice of Life

Container: bread bag

Materials: white and brown paper

Preparation:

1. Using the pattern, cut out two brown and twenty white slices of bread.

2. On one brown slice write **Living**, and on the other write **Nonliving**. Number these **1** and **2**.

3. On each of ten white slices write the name of a living thing, and on each of the ten others write the name of a nonliving thing.

   Suggested word list:

bear	flower	sheep	glass	tire
cow	grass	tree	house	wall
dog	man	car	jar	window
fish	mouse	clothes	stone	wire

4. For self-checking, number the backs of the white slices to match brown slices.

Directions: Set out the brown slices of bread. Sort the matching white slices of bread under them.

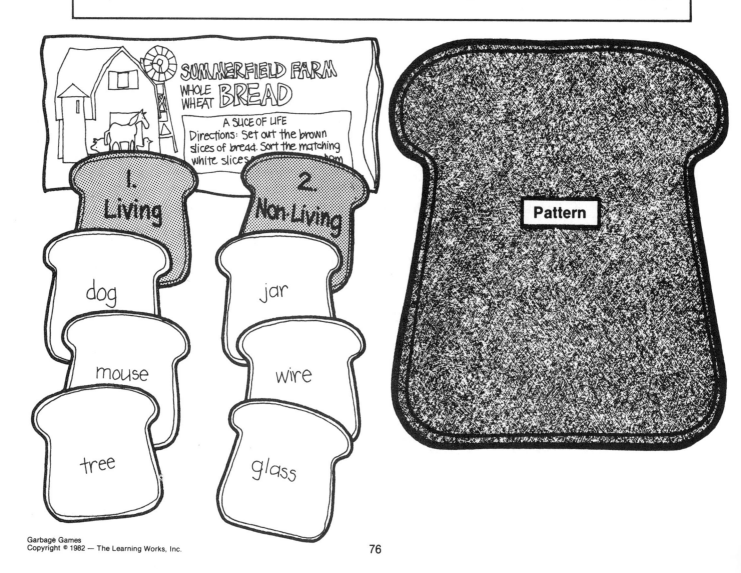

Dipping into Directions

Container: ice cream carton

Materials: paper in assorted colors, including white

Preparation:
1. Using the patterns, cut out three white bowls and nine ice cream dips of assorted colors.
2. Number the bowls **1**, **2**, and **3**.
3. Write one of these directions on each ice cream dip:

   Place this dip in bowl 1.
   Place this dip in bowl 2.
   Place this dip in bowl 3.
   Place this dip on top of another dip in any bowl.
   Place this dip on the right side of bowl 3.
   Place this dip on the left side of bowl 2.
   Place this dip above bowl 2.
   Place this dip on bowl 3.
   Keep this dip in your hand.

4. This game can be checked by a friend.

Directions: Set out the bowls. Follow the directions on the ice cream dips. Have a friend check your work.

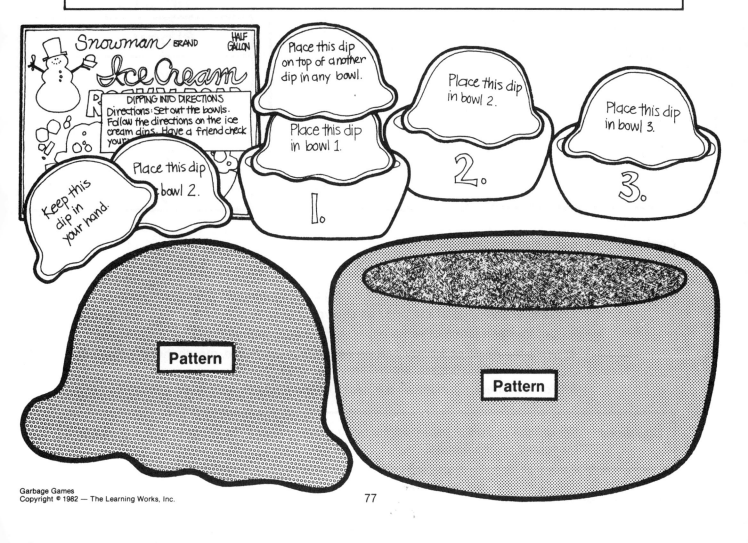

Milkman

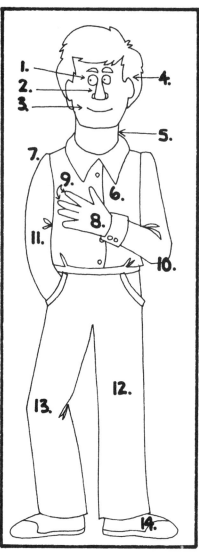

| eye |
| nose |
| mouth |
| head |
| neck |
| chest |
| shoulder |
| hand |
| fingers |
| elbow |
| arm |
| leg |
| knee |
| foot |

Container: quart-sized paper milk carton

Materials: white paper and old magazines

Preparation: 1. Cut a picture of a person out of a magazine and mount it on white paper.
2. Number the parts of the body as shown.
3. Cut fourteen strips of white paper, each measuring one inch by four inches.
4. Write the name of a body part on each strip: **eye**, **nose**, **mouth**, **head**, **neck**, **chest**, **shoulder**, **hand**, **fingers**, **elbow**, **arm**, **leg**, **knee**, or **foot**.
5. For self-checking, number the backs of the strips to match the picture.

Directions: Set out the picture. Line up all the body parts to match the order in which they are numbered on the picture.

Clay Colors

Container: clay can

Materials: red, orange, yellow, green, blue, purple, white, brown, and black paper

Preparation: 1. From paper of each color, cut one circle two inches in diameter. Cut ten white strips, each measuring one inch by three inches.

2. On each strip, write the name of a color.

3. For self-checking, put the same number on the back of the circle and strip in each correctly matched pair.

Directions: Line up the colored circles. Match the color words to them.

green

orange

brown

blue

white

purple

yellow

red

black

Rainbow Riddles

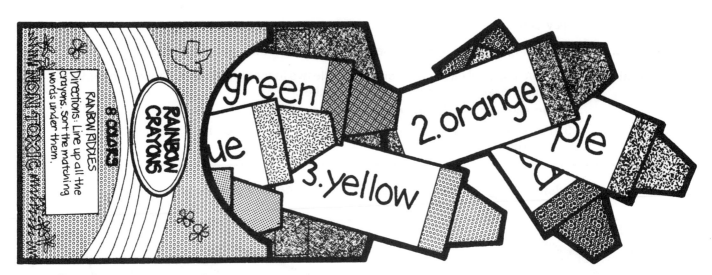

Container: crayon box

Materials: red, orange, yellow, green, blue, purple, white, brown, and black paper

Preparation:
1. Using the pattern, cut out eight crayons (one of each color). Cut out thirty-two white strips of paper, each measuring one inch by three inches.
2. Number the crayons **1** through **8**.
3. On each crayon write the color of the crayon.
4. On each of the strips write the name of an object commonly associated with that color.

   Suggested word list:

   red — beet, blood, cherry
   orange — carrot, orange, pumpkin
   yellow — banana, butter, sun
   green — bushes, frog, leaves
   blue — jeans, sky, water
   purple — grape juice, plum, violet
   brown — chocolate, cookie, peanut
   black — coal, tire, witch's hat
5. For self-checking, number the backs of the strips to match the crayons.

Directions: Line up all the crayons. Sort the matching words under them.

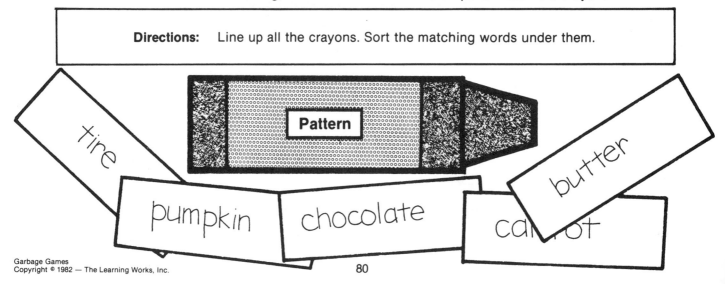

Colossal Cleaning

Container: detergent bottle or box

Materials: white and blue paper

Preparation: 1. Cut ten white and ten blue strips, each measuring one inch by four inches.

2. On each blue strip, write the name of an object to be cleaned.

3. On each white strip, write the name of a product or item that is used to clean one of these objects.

   Suggest word list:

bathtub, cleanser	person, soap
boot, shoe polish	rug, vacuum cleaner
clothes, detergent	table, dust cloth
floor, broom (or mop)	teeth, toothpaste
paintbrush, turpentine	yard, rake

4. For self-checking, put the same number on the back of the blue strip and the white strip of each correctly matched pair.

Directions: Line up all the blue strips. Match a white strip with each blue one.

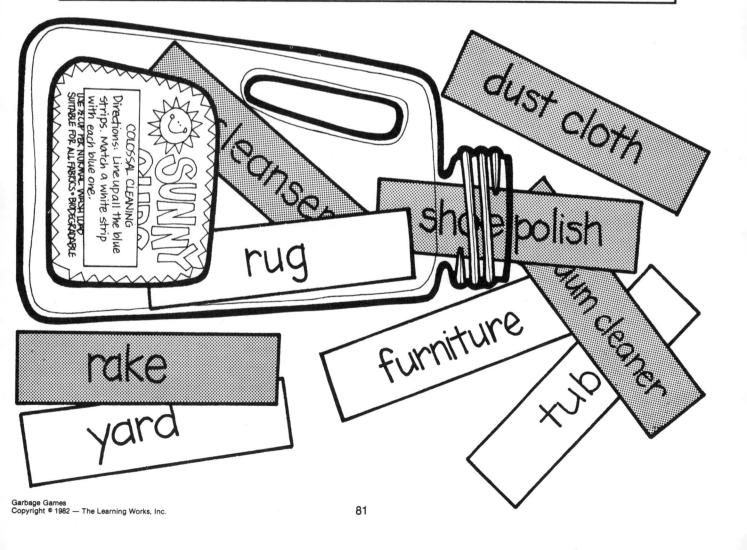

Sorta Soft

Container:	marshmallow cream jar or marshmallow bag
Materials:	white and pink paper
Preparation:	1. Using the pattern, cut out twenty white and two pink marshmallows.

2. On one pink marshmallow write **soft**, and on the other write **hard**. Number these **1** and **2**.

3. On each of the white marshmallows write the name of an object that is hard or soft.

   Suggested word list:

bunny	fur	snowflake	floor	stone
cloud	marshmallow	sponge	glass	street
cotton	quilt	brick	rock	tree
feather	pillow	cement	steel	wood

4. For self-checking, number the backs of the white marshmallows to match the pink ones.

Directions: Set out the pink marshmallows. Sort the white marshmallows under them.

Prune Face

Container:	prune jar or box
Materials:	brown paper and magazine pictures of people
Preparation:	1. Using the pattern, cut out twenty-two prunes.
	2. On one prune write **Happy**, and on the other write **Not Happy**. Number these **1** and **2**.
	3. From magazines, cut out twenty pictures of happy and unhappy faces (may be angry, sad, etc.).
	4. Glue the faces on the twenty remaining prunes.
	5. For self-checking, number the backs of the picture prunes to match the category prunes.

Directions: Set out the **Happy** and **Not Happy** prunes. Sort the prune faces under them.

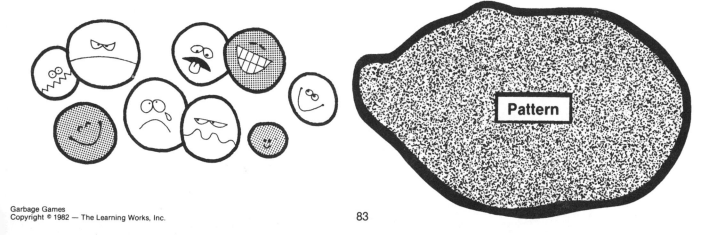

Toasted Traits

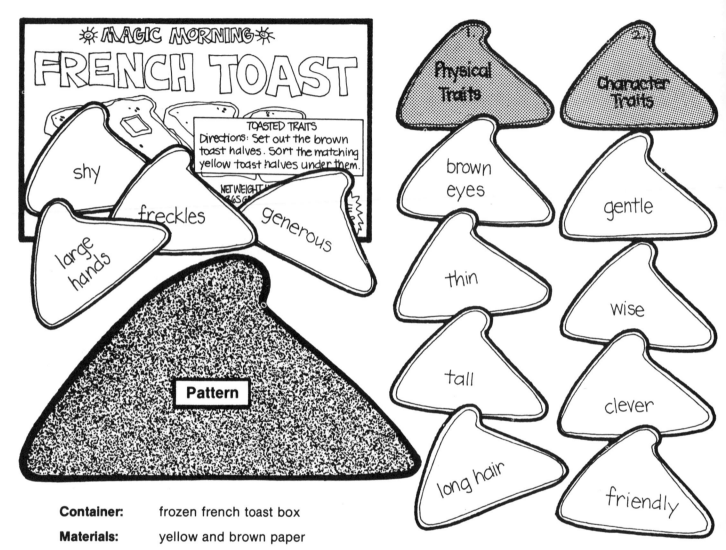

Container: frozen french toast box

Materials: yellow and brown paper

Preparation:
1. Using the pattern, cut out two brown and twenty yellow toast halves.
2. On one brown toast half write **Physical Traits**, and on the other write **Character Traits**. Number these **1** and **2**.
3. On ten yellow toast halves write physical traits and on ten others write character traits.

   Suggested trait list:

fat	blond hair	rosy cheeks	generous	nice
short	blue eyes	small ears	gentle	selfish
tall	fair skin	clever	kind	thoughtful
thin	long fingers	foolish	mean	wise

4. For self-checking, number the backs of the yellow toast halves to match the brown ones.

Directions: Set out the brown toast halves. Sort the matching yellow toast halves under them.

Graham Cracker Guide Words

Container: graham cracker box

Materials: brown and white paper

Preparation:
1. Using the pattern, cut out twenty brown graham crackers.
2. Cut out three white strips, each measuring two inches by four inches.
3. On the first white strip write **Comes between apple and jam**, on the second white strip write **Comes between kite and pin**, and on the third white strip write **Comes between quick and zoo**. Number the strips **1**, **2**, and **3**.
4. On each graham cracker write a word that would be found on the pages with these guide words.

   Suggested word list:

banana	ghost	never	stale
camel	heart	over	time
dog	land	pen	under
elephant	man	quiet	van
flower	neat	rail	wash

5. For self-checking, number the backs of the graham crackers to match the white guide word strips.

Directions: Set out the white guide word strips. Sort the graham crackers under them.

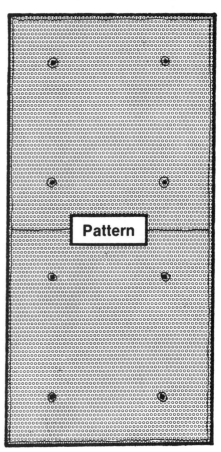

Coffee Cans

Container: coffee can

Material: brown paper

Preparation:
1. Using the pattern, cut out twenty-six drops of coffee.
2. Print a letter of the alphabet on each drop.
3. For self-checking, number the backs of the drops in alphabetical order.

Directions: Line up all the coffee drops in ABC order.

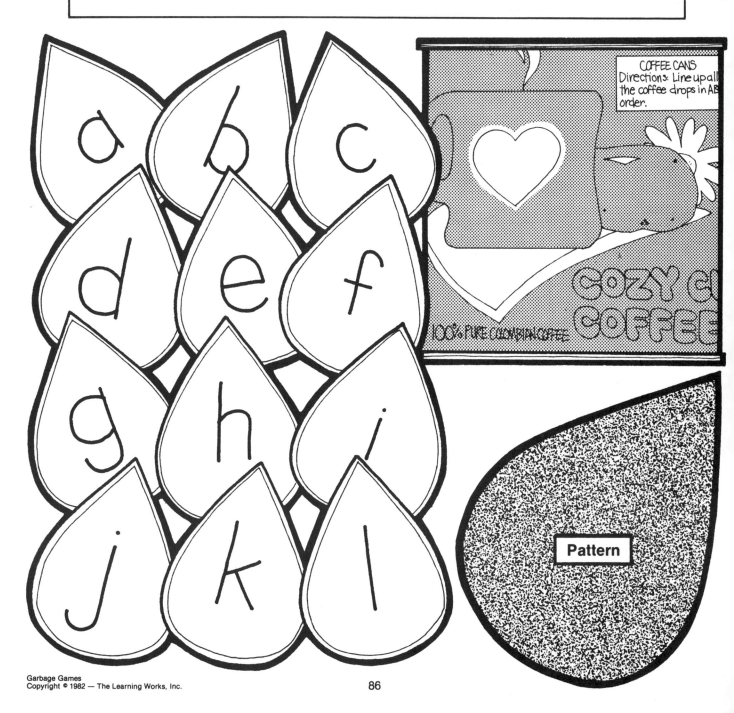

Iced T

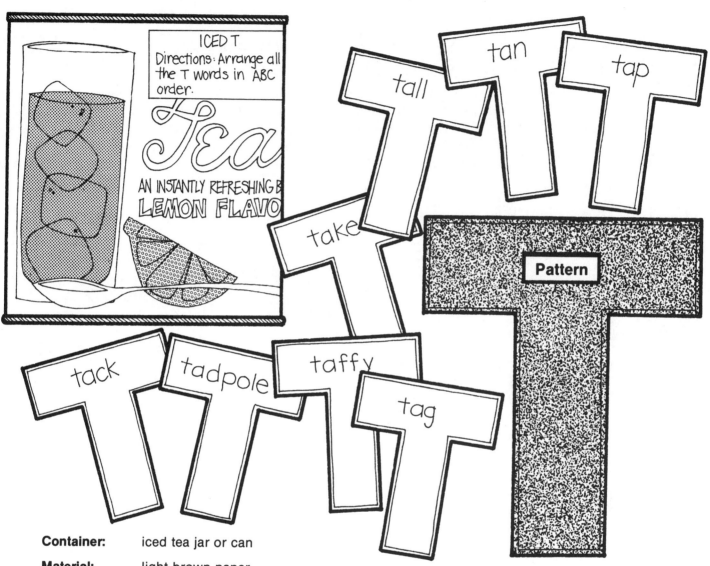

ICED T
Directions: Arrange all the T words in ABC order.

Tea

AN INSTANTLY REFRESHING B
LEMON FLAVO

tall · tan · tap · take

Pattern

tack · tadpole · taffy · tag

Container:	iced tea jar or can
Material:	light brown paper
Preparation:	1. Using the pattern, cut out twelve **T** shapes.
	2. Write a word beginning with **t** on each one.

Suggested word list:

tab	take
tack	tall
tadpole	tam
taffy	tan
tag	tap
tail	taste

3. For self-checking, number the backs of the **T**s in alphabetical order.

Directions: Arrange all the **T** words in ABC order.

Taco Talk

Container: taco shell box

Materials: light brown and yellow paper, and crayons or felt-tipped pens

Preparation:
1. Using the patterns, cut out ten brown taco shells and ten yellow taco fillings.
2. Color the top of the filling green and the bottom brown.
3. Fold the shells on the dotted lines, and write a word on the outside of each one. Use words at the appropriate reading level.
4. Write the pronunciation respellings on the fillings.
5. For self-checking, number the backs of matching sets.

Directions: To make tacos, set out the taco shells. Put the right filling in each taco.

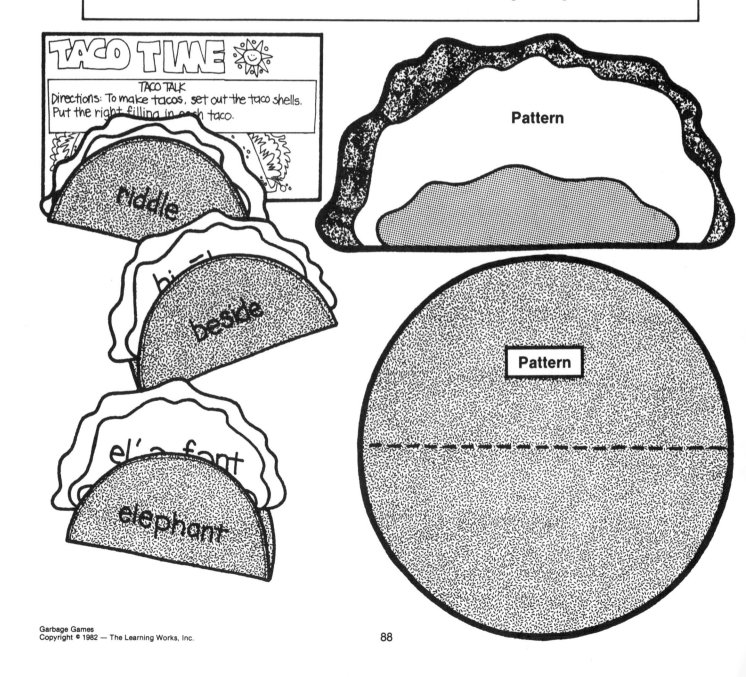

Dine on Definitions

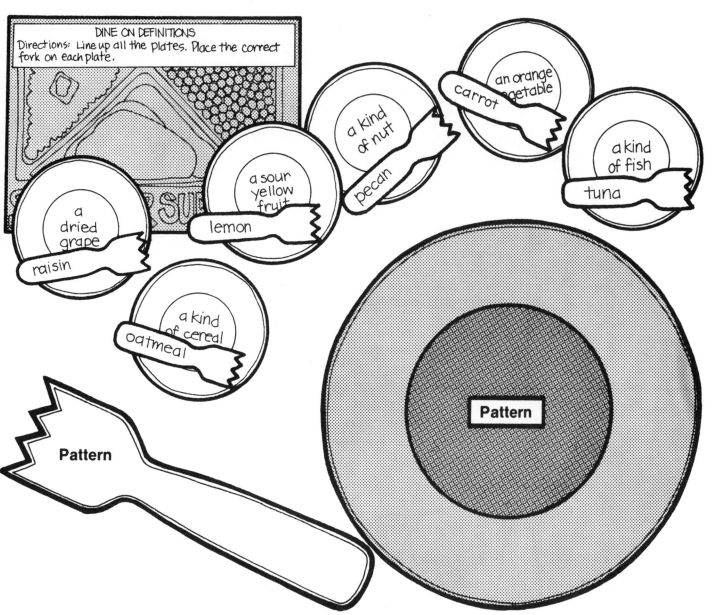

DINE ON DEFINITIONS
Directions: Line up all the plates. Place the correct fork on each plate.

a dried grape — raisin

a sour yellow fruit — lemon

a kind of nut — pecan

an orange vegetable — carrot

a kind of fish — tuna

a kind of cereal — oatmeal

Pattern

Pattern

Container: frozen dinner box

Materials: red and white paper

Preparation:
1. Using the patterns, cut out twenty red plates and twenty white forks.
2. On each fork write an easily defined word. Use words at the appropriate reading level.
3. On each plate write one of the definitions.
4. For self-checking, number the backs of matching sets.

Directions: Line up all the plates. Place the correct fork on each plate.

Cupful of Clues

Container: paper cup box

Materials: paper in assorted pastel colors and clear plastic bingo disks

Preparation: 1. Using the pattern, cut out ten paper cups of assorted colors.

2. On each cup, write a sentence containing a key word and other words that describe or help the reader determine its meaning. Underline the key word.

Suggested sentence list:

We **bounced** the big **round** <u>ball</u>.
In our <u>boat</u>, we **traveled** across the **water**.
Mary made **music** by **strumming** the **strings** of her <u>guitar</u>.
In the <u>fireplace</u>, the **log burned** brightly.
We saw the <u>lightning</u> **flash** across the **sky** and heard the **thunder** rumble.
Forcing **air** through the **pipes** of an organ causes it to make **musical sounds**.
Many **people** came to **eat** and have <u>fun</u> at my <u>party</u>.
We dug **holes** in the **ground** to <u>plant</u> **seeds**.
In the **evening**, Sue **ate** a **salad** for <u>supper</u>.
The **glass** <u>window</u> lets in **light**.

3. For self-checking, write the words that are clues on the back of each paper cup. For your convenience, clue words in the sentences above have been set in boldface type.

Directions: Set out the paper cups. Place a disk on each word in a sentence that gives you a clue about the meaning of the underlined word in that sentence.

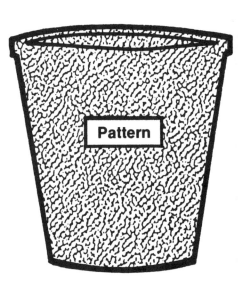

Lemonade Look-Alikes

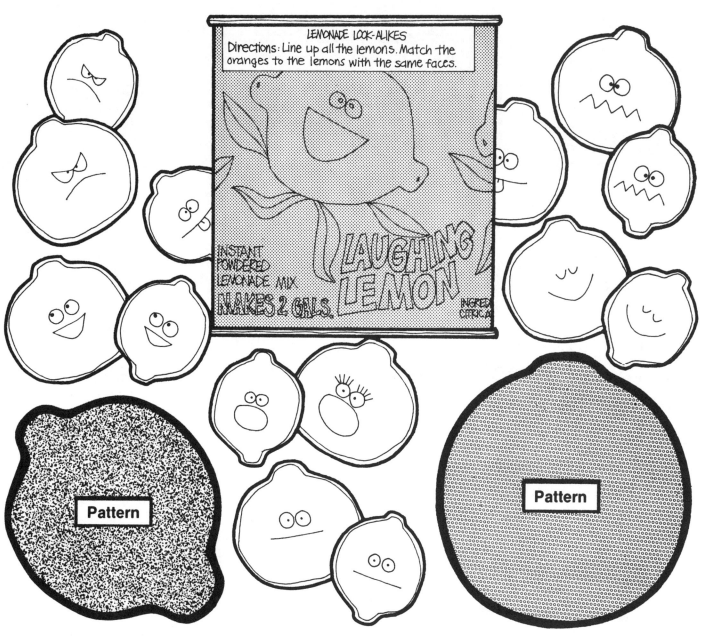

Container: frozen or powdered lemonade can

Materials: yellow and orange paper

Preparation:
1. Using the patterns, cut out twelve lemons and twelve oranges.
2. Pair up lemons with oranges.
3. Draw identical eyes and mouths on each pair.
4. For self-checking, number the backs of matching sets.

Directions: Line up all the lemons. Match the oranges to the lemons with the same faces.

Cut-Ups

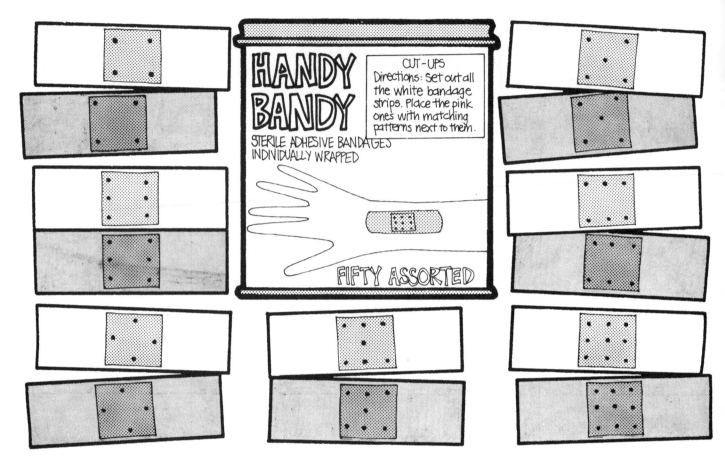

Container:	bandage box
Materials:	pink and white paper
Preparation:	1. Using the pattern, cut out twelve pink and twelve white bandage strips.
	2. Draw lines to indicate the gauze portion of each bandage strip.
	3. On each pink bandage strip, draw a different pattern of dots to indicate breathing holes.
	4. On the white strips, draw dot patterns to match those drawn on the pink strips.
	5. For self-checking, number the backs of matching sets.

Directions: Set out all the white bandage strips. Place the pink ones with matching patterns next to them.

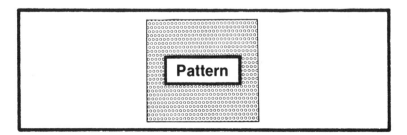

Candle Quiz

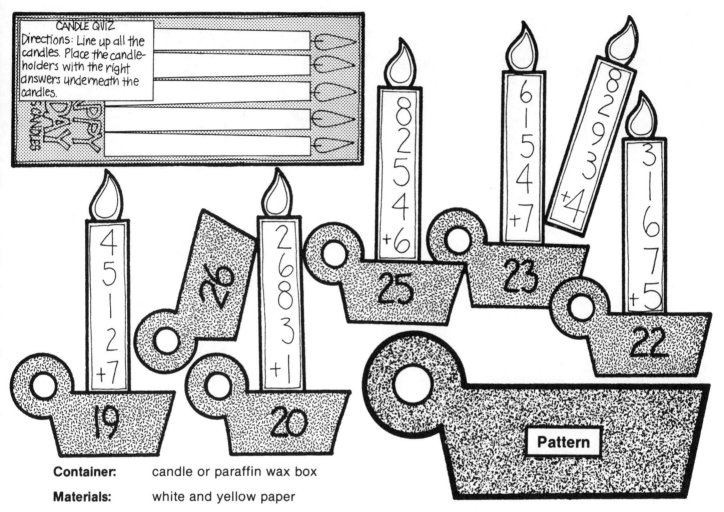

Container:	candle or paraffin wax box
Materials:	white and yellow paper
Preparation:	1. Using the patterns, cut out fifteen white candles and fifteen yellow candleholders.
	2. Write columnar addition problems on the candles. Use problems at the appropriate math level.
	3. Write the answers on the candleholders.
	4. For self-checking, put the same letter on the back of the candle and candleholder in each correctly matched pair.

Directions: Line up all the candles. Place the candleholders with the right answers underneath the candles.

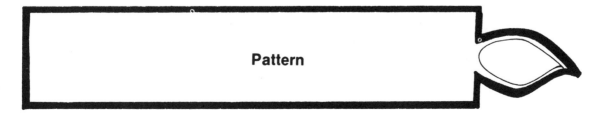

Pattern

Soup Sums

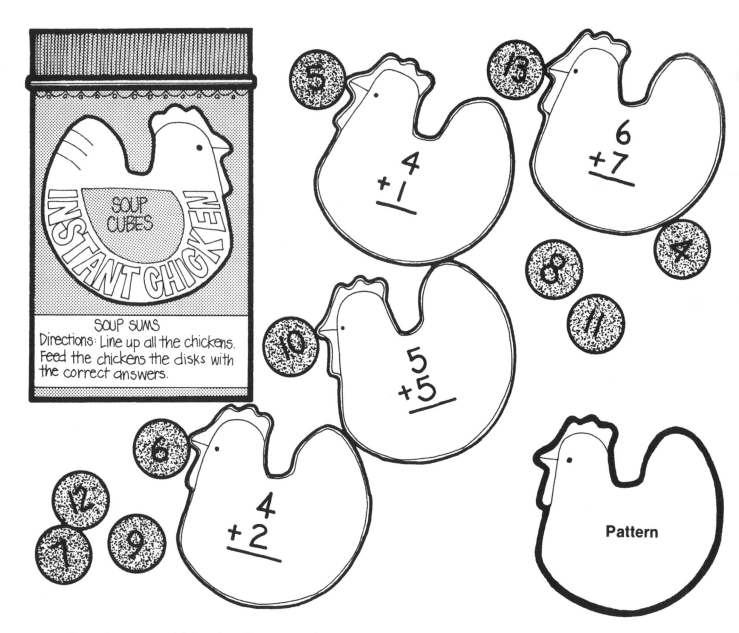

Container: chicken bouillon can or jar

Materials: white paper, a permanent marking pen, and clear plastic bingo disks

Preparation:
1. Using the pattern, cut out twenty chickens.
2. Write an addition problem on each chicken. Use problems at the appropriate math level.
3. Using a permanent marking pen, write the answers to the problems on the disks.
4. For self-checking, write the answers on the backs of the chickens.

Directions: Line up all the chickens. Feed the chickens the disks with the correct answers.

Pizza Plus

Container: frozen pizza box

Materials: cardboard pizza plate, yellow paper, and crayons or felt-tipped pens

Preparation:
1. Draw lines on the pizza plate to indicate eight segments.
2. Cut eight pieces of "pizza" from the yellow paper to fit the segments on the plate.
3. Color each piece to look like pizza.
4. Write a number in each of the three corners of each piece of pizza. Use addition problems at the appropriate math level.
5. Write the sum of these numbers in a pizza plate segment.
6. For self-checking, write the sum of the numbers on the back of each pizza piece.

Directions: Set out the pizza plate. Add the numbers on the pizza pieces and put them in the correct places on the plate.

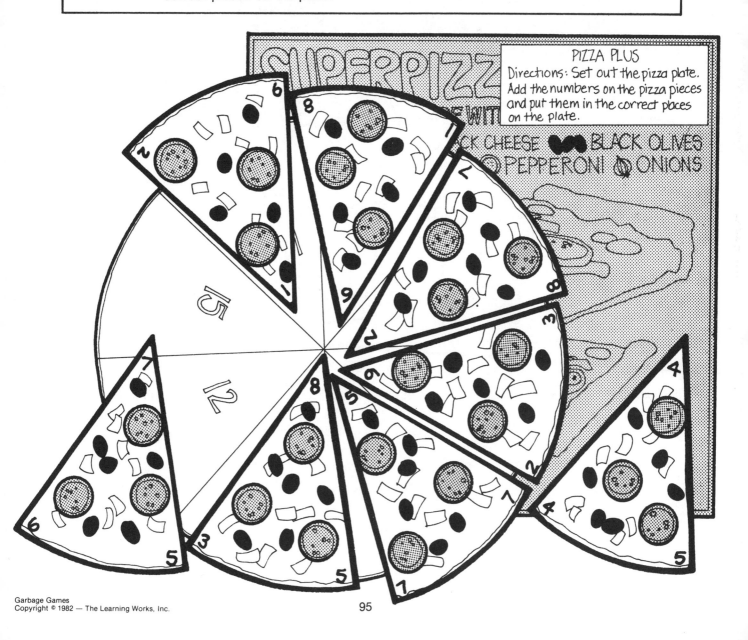

I Scream for Ice Cream

I SCREAM FOR ICE CREAM
Directions: Line up all the cones. Put ice cream dips with the right answers on top of them.

CONES
...A PARTY IN EVERY BOX...

TWENTY CONES

Container: ice cream cone box

Materials: light brown and pastel-colored paper

Preparation:
1. Using the patterns, cut out twenty light brown cones and twenty colored ice cream dips.
2. Write double-digit addition problems on the cones. Use problems at the appropriate math level.
3. Write the answers to these problems on the ice cream dips.
4. For self-checking, put the same letter on the back of the cone and ice cream dip in each correctly matched set.

Directions: Line up all the cones. Put the ice cream dips with the right answers on top of them.

Egg-sactly Right

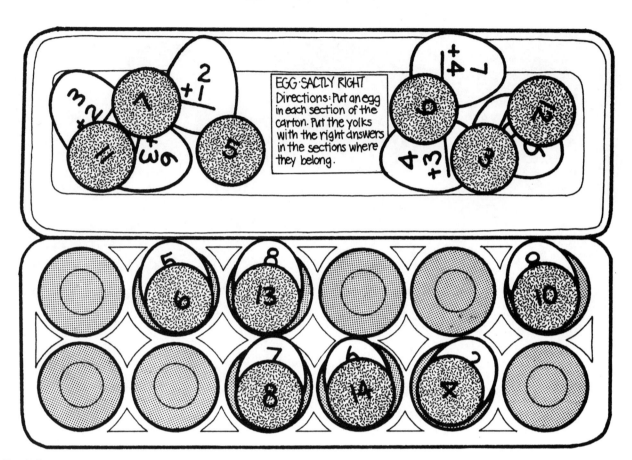

Container: egg carton

Materials: white and yellow paper

Preparation:
1. Using the patterns, cut out twelve white eggs and twelve yellow yolks.
2. Write addition problems on the eggs. Use problems at the appropriate math level.
3. Write the answers on the yolks.
4. For self-checking, put the same letter on the back of the egg and yolk in each correctly matched set.

Directions: Put an egg in each section of the carton. Put the yolks with the right answers in the sections where they belong.

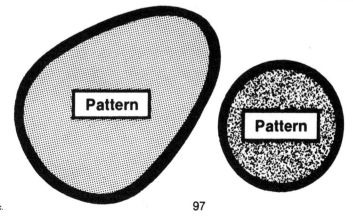

Dandy Candy

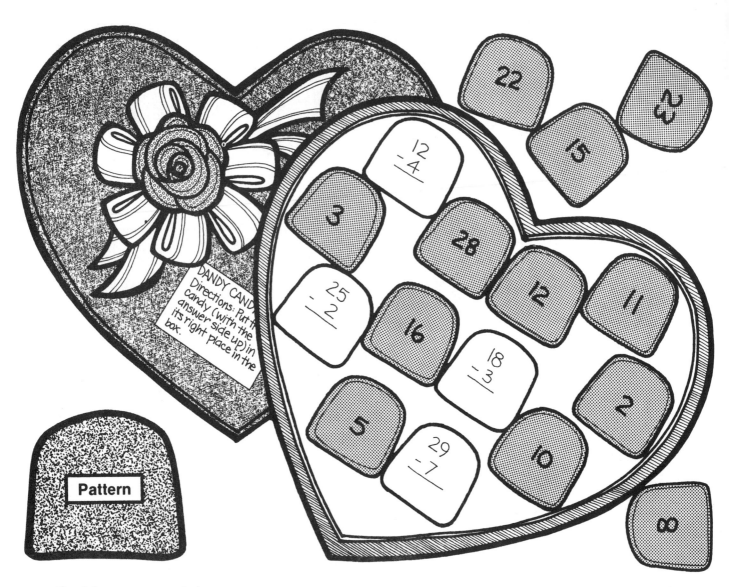

Container: candy box

Material: brown paper

Preparation:
1. Using the pattern, trace twelve pieces of candy in the bottom half of the box.
2. Using the pattern, cut twelve pieces of candy from brown paper.
3. Within the outline of each piece of candy in the box, write a subtraction problem. Use problems at the appropriate math level.
4. Write the answers to these problems on separate pieces of candy.
5. For self-checking, write the corresponding math problem on the back of each piece of candy.

Directions: Put the candy (with the answer side up) in its right place in the box.

Twice the Headache

Container: large aspirin bottle

Materials: white and yellow paper

Preparation:
1. Cut out twelve yellow and twelve white circles, each measuring one inch in diameter.
2. On each white circle, write a number from **1** through **12**.
3. On the yellow circles, write the products of these numbers when multiplied by two.
4. For self-checking, letter the backs of matching sets.

Directions: Set out all the white aspirin tablets. Multiply the number on each tablet by two. Match the yellow aspirin tablets with the white ones.

Donut Division

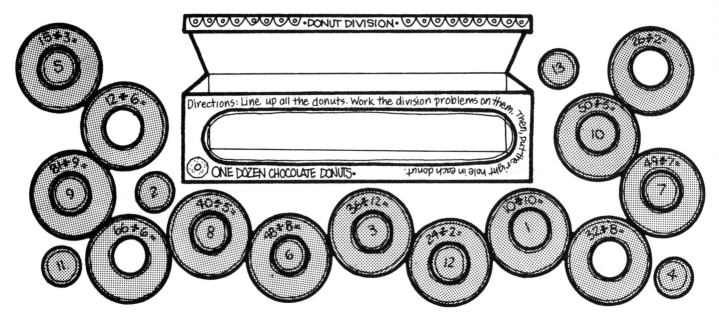

Container: small donut box

Materials: dark brown and light brown paper

Preparation:
1. Using the patterns, cut out fifteen donut shapes and fifteen donut holes.
2. Write a division problem on each donut.
3. Write the answers to these problems on the donut holes.
4. For self-checking, put the same letter on the backs of matching sets.

Directions: Line up all the donuts. Work the division problems on them. Then, put the right hole in each donut.

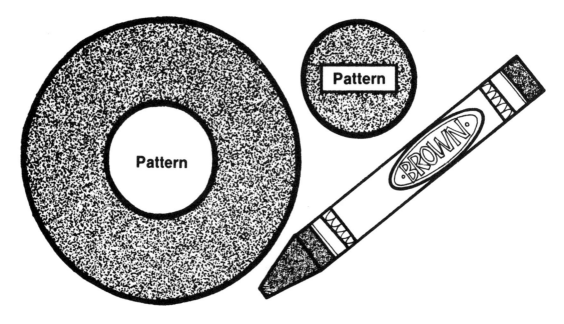

Pinch an Inch

Container: diet sugar box

Material: pink paper

Preparation: 1. Using the pattern, cut out one pig for each child.

                     2. Write **six inches** on each pig, and draw a ruler to indicate the length of the pig.

Directions: Use a pig to measure ten things around you. Record your findings on a piece of paper.

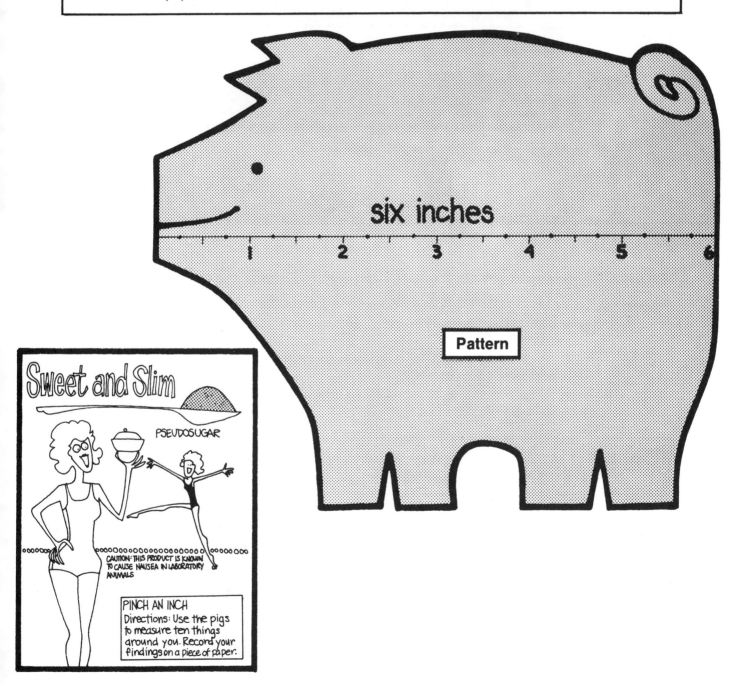

Pattern

Matchless Meters

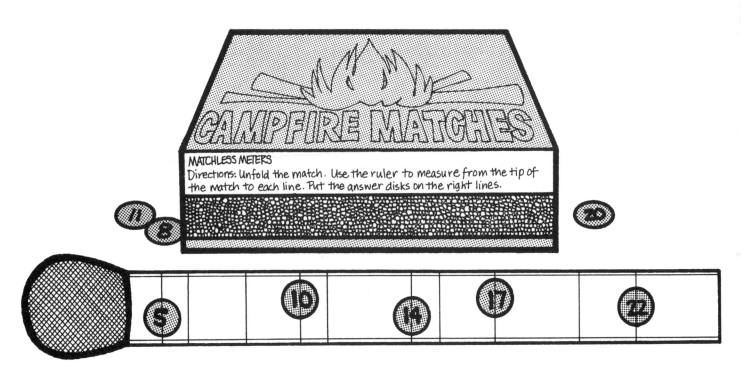

Container:	match box
Materials:	centimeter ruler, white paper, clear plastic bingo disks, and crayons or felt-tipped pens

Preparation:

1. Using the pattern, cut out one large match and extend the length to eighteen inches.
2. Draw lines across the match at random, yet distinct, centimeter lengths, and color the match tip.
3. On the bingo disks, write the various centimeter measurements you used from the tip of the match to each line.
4. For self-checking, write the measurements on the back of the match at the position of each line.

Directions:	Unfold the match. Use the ruler to measure from the tip of the match to each line. Put the answer disks on the right lines.

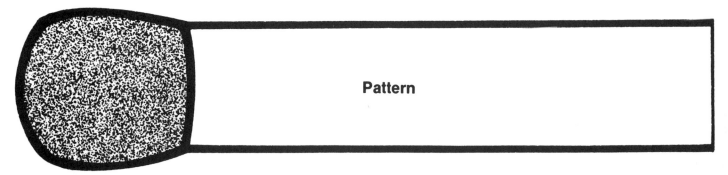

Pattern

Line Up

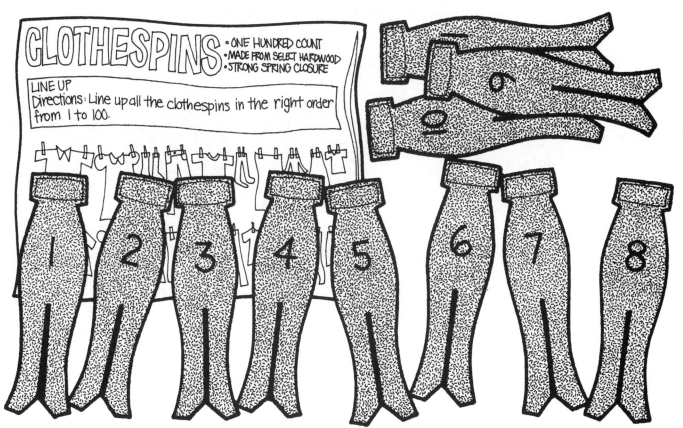

Container: clothespin container

Materials: assorted colored paper

Preparation:
1. Using the pattern, cut out and mark one hundred assorted colored clothespins.
2. Number the clothespins from **1** through **100**.
3. To check, have children compare their arranged clothespins with a posted number line.

Directions: Line up all the clothespins in the right order from **1** to **100**.

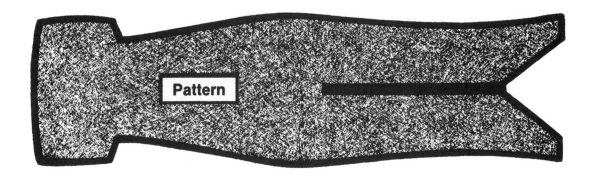

Nuts-and-Bolts Numbers

Container: nuts-and-bolts box

Material: white paper

Preparation:
1. Using the patterns, cut out twenty nuts and twenty bolts.
2. On each bolt, write a sequence of three numbers, omitting the middle number in the sequence.
3. Write the missing numbers on the nuts.
4. For self-checking, put the same letter on the backs of the matching nuts and bolts.

Directions: Line up all the bolts. Match up the nuts with the missing numbers.

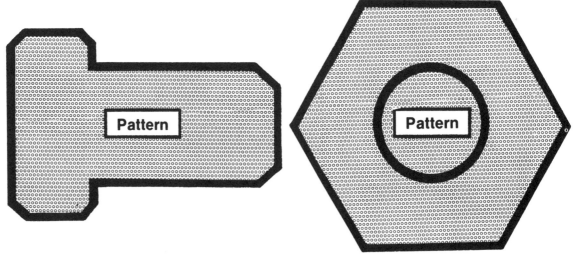

Paper Dolls

DAISY DOLLS

23   31

PAPER DOLLS
Directions: Make a paper doll chain.
Arrange the dolls in order from the
smallest to the largest number.

Pattern

Container: doll box

Materials: assorted colored paper

Preparation: 1. Using the pattern, cut out twenty-five dolls in assorted colors.

2. Number the dolls from **1** to **49**, using odd numbers only.

3. For self-checking, letter the backs of the dolls in alphabetical order.

Directions:	Make a paper doll chain. Arrange the dolls in order from the smallest to the largest number.

Honey Money

eight dollars
and five cents

$8.05

one hundred
dollars

$100.00

HARMONY
HONEY

PRODUCED IN HARMONY, CALIFORNIA
A SAGE & WILDFLOWER BLEND

HONEY MONEY
Directions: Line up all
the orange bees. Match
up the yellow bees
with them.

twenty
dollars

$20.00

eighty-
five cents

85¢

Container: honey jar

Materials: yellow and orange paper, black felt-tipped marking pen or crayon

Preparation:
1. Using the pattern, cut out ten yellow and ten orange bees.
2. Draw eyes on the bees and blacken the antennae.
3. On the orange bees, write an expression of cash value, such as $100.00, 42¢, $1.20, and so on, in numerals and signs.
4. On the yellow bees, write the same values entirely in words.
5. For self-checking, write the same letter on the back of the yellow bee and orange bee in each correctly matched set.

Directions: Line up all the orange bees. Match up the yellow bees with them.

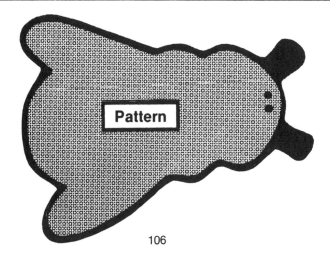

Pattern

Super Cents

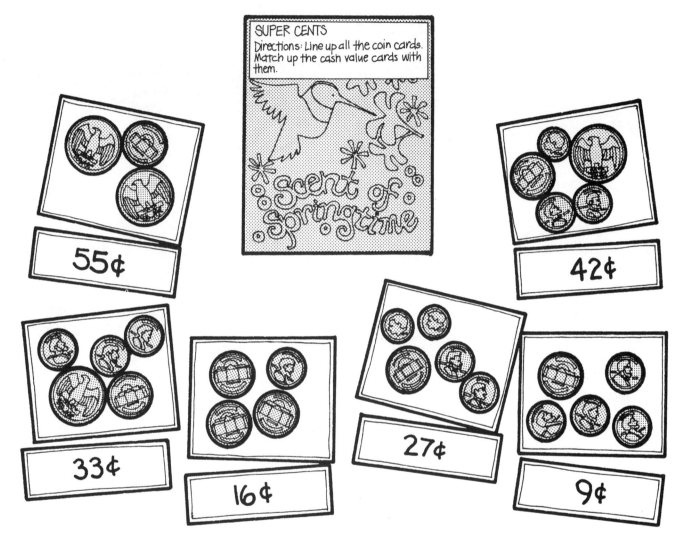

Container: four-by-six-inch perfume box

Materials: three-by-five-inch index cards; cardboard; nickels, dimes, quarters, and pennies; and clear Contact paper

Preparation:
1. Cut ten cardboard rectangles, each measuring one inch by four inches.
2. Write letters from **A** through **J** on the backs of the index cards.
3. Arrange different combinations of coins on the fronts of the index cards and cover with clear Contact paper.
4. Write the cash value of each combination on a rectangle.
5. For self-checking, letter the backs of the rectangles to match the cards.

Directions: Line up all the coin cards. Match up the cash value cards with them.

Raisin Guess-timation

Container:	raisin cereal box
Materials:	small plastic bags, raisins, brown paper, and felt-tipped marking pen
Preparation:	1. Count various amounts of raisins into ten plastic bags and seal.
	2. Using the pattern, cut out ten paper raisins.
	3. On each paper raisin, write the amount of raisins found in each bag.
	4. For self-checking, letter the bags and the backs of the paper raisins to indicate matching sets.

Directions: Estimate the number of raisins in each bag. Put the paper raisin with your guess by each bag.

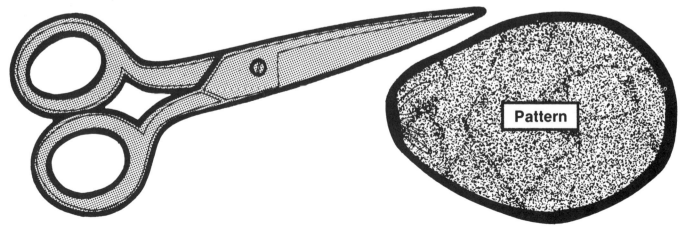

Pretzel Time

Container:	pretzel box or can
Materials:	three-by-five-inch index cards, brown paper, and felt-tipped marking pen or stamp of clock face (optional)
Preparation:	1. Draw or stamp clock faces on ten index cards.
	2. Draw hands on clock faces to indicate different times.
	3. Using the pattern, cut out ten brown pretzels.
	4. Draw dots on the pretzels to suggest salt.
	5. On the pretzels write the times indicated by the clocks.
	6. For self-checking, write the same letter on the back of the pretzel and clock face card in each correctly matched set.

Directions: Line up all the clocks. Match the pretzel times with them.

Pattern

Math Munchies

Container: cracker box

Materials: yellow and orange paper and black felt-tipped marking pen

Preparation: 1. Using the pattern, cut out seven orange and seven yellow crackers.

2. On the orange crackers write math vocabulary words.

   Suggested word list:

add	is equal to
subtract	is greater than
multiply	is less than
divide	

3. On the yellow crackers write the symbols for these words. Put a dot below each symbol near the bottom of the cracker.

4. For self-checking, write the same letter on the back of the orange cracker and the yellow cracker in each correctly matched set.

Directions: Line up the orange crackers. Turn the yellow crackers so that the dots are at the bottom. Match the yellow crackers with the orange ones.

110

Taking a Shine to Signs

Container: shoe polish can

Materials: white and red paper and black felt-tipped marking pen

Preparation:
1. Cut twenty white strips, each measuring one and one-half inches by four inches.
2. Cut twenty red one-inch squares.
3. Write two numbers on the white strips, leaving space between them for the missing sign (< or >).
4. On the squares, write the missing signs. Put a dot below each sign near the bottom of the square.
5. For self-checking, rewrite the inequality on the back of each strip and include the correct sign.

Directions: Line up the number strips. Turn the squares so that the dots are at the bottom. Place the square with the right sign between the numbers on each strip.

Ship-Shape Sandwiches

circle   cone   square

SHIP-SHAPE SANDWICHES
Directions: Set out all the sandwiches. Match the strip with the right shape name with each sandwich.

Container: lunch box

Materials: brown paper, white paper, and brown crayon or felt-tipped marking pen

Preparation: 1. Using the pattern, cut out eight brown sandwiches.
                   2. Color the sandwich filling.
                   3. Cut eight strips of white paper, each measuring one and one-half inches by four inches.
                   4. Draw one of the following shapes on each sandwich: circle, square, rectangle, triangle, cone, cylinder, cube, or octagon.
                   5. Write the names of the shapes on the strips.
                   6. For self-checking, number the backs of matching sets.

Directions: Set out all the sandwiches. Match the strip with the right shape name with each sandwich.

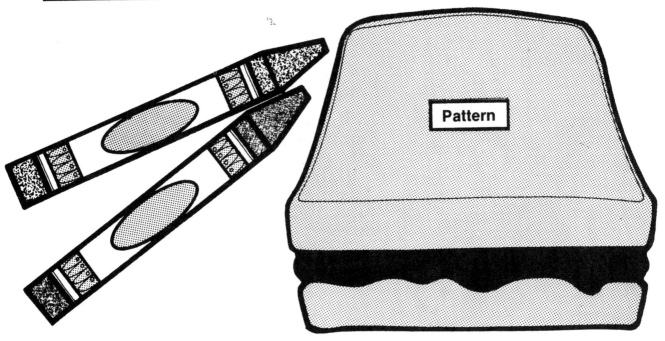

Pattern